ASSAULT ON ST NAZAIRE

ASSAULT ON ST NAZAIRE

Duncan Harding

SEVERN SH HOUSE

This first world edition published in Great Britain 1997 by
SEVERN HOUSE PUBLISHERS LTD of
9–15 High Street, Sutton, Surrey SM1 1DF.
First published in the U.S.A. 1997 by
SEVERN HOUSE PUBLISHERS INC. of
595 Madison Avenue, New York, NY 10022.

British Library Cataloguing in Publication Data
Harding, Duncan
    Assault on St Nazaire
    1.World War, 1939–1945 – Fiction 2.War stories
    I. Title
    823.9′14[F]

    ISBN 0-7278-5129-2

Typeset by Hewer Text Composition Services, Edinburgh.
Printed and bound in Great Britain by
Hartnolls Ltd, Bodmin, Cornwall.

BOOK ONE

THE HARD MAN

Chapter One

"Busy?" the Hard Man rasped in that harsh, grating voice of his. Hastily he addded, "*Matey.*" He knew he had a pronounced accent, but he had learned, since he had begun to practise his little deception on the Tommies, to add the kind of words they used – 'matey', 'ducks', 'old lad' and the like – so that these uneducated British dockers would forget his accent and the dyed blue battledress with the round brown patches which indicated that he was an enemy prisoner of war.

"Ay," the elderly docker with the mouthful of rotten teeth and a half-smoked Woodbine perched behind his right ear, agreed. "Not been as busy as this for bleedin' years. And there's plenty of overtime as well." He hitched up his faded, torn dungarees and stared at Southampton Water below.

Traffic, naval and civilian, stretched as far as the eye could see. It seemed the ships were so tightly crammed together that one could walk from ship to ship right across the anchorage without putting a foot in the water.

There were the usual coasters which had run the gauntlet of the German tip-and-run raiders from France; listing freighters which had survived the terrible Atlantic run from the States, their decks still littered with empty shell-casings; a tanker, listed heavily to port, smoke

3

pouring from its ruptured engines, men from the Auxiliary Fire Service spraying it constantly with water from giant hosepipes to prevent the flames from spreading.

Hard Man rejoiced inwardly, though his scarred face revealed nothing of his emotions. The 'Big Lion', as his U-boat crews called Admiral Doenitz, head of the U-boat Army, was really hitting the Tommies hard where it hurt in their guts. Hardly any food was getting through from the States to hard-pressed Britain. At this rate, the Tommies would soon have to throw in the towel and surrender to the Führer, Adolf Hitler. Still, Hard Man told himself, as a flotilla of strange flat-prowed craft started to make their way through the packed traffic, the day when that drunken Jewish sod Churchill asked abjectly for surrender terms had not yet arrived, unfortunately.

"Commandos," the ancient docker said, as if he could read Hard Man's thoughts as the latter puzzled over the awkward-looking camouflaged craft. "Full of piss and vinegar they are! Tough lot. Allus wrecking the boozers when the landlord sez he's run outa beer so that he can sell it – gnat's piss, as it is – to the Canadians, and getting the local lasses up the spout more than likely," he added darkly. "Nice lads all the same. Win the war for us, I don't doubt."

"Commandos?" Hard Man asked, slightly puzzled. Whatever happened in the next few weeks, even if the Tommies had surrendered by then, he wanted to take back all the information he could to the Homeland. Naval Intelligence would be grateful, for every crumb.

"Yer, old Winnie set them up last year," the old dockie informed me. "Said they'd put the wind up the Hun."

Hard Man winced at the word. Why didn't the Tommies use 'German'? It wasn't fair. They *weren't* 'Huns'.

4

"Yer," the old man said, taking the precious cigarette end from behind his dirty ear, "it looks to me as if the lads are getting ready to have another crack at the Old Hun like they did in Norway last year."

There it was again. Hard Man hoped the old fart would choke on the smoke of his rotten Woodbine.

Vaguely the docker gestured in the general direction of the German-occupied Continent. "Give 'im a bloody nose till old Winnie sees 'em off for friggin' good."

"How do you mean, old lad?" he asked, remembering to use the colloquial expression.

Now, vaguely, he started to become aware of the steady throb of fast aircraft engines in the distance over the sea. Somewhere in the bombed, ruined port, grey smoke still curling upwards from the previous night's raid, sirens began to wail mournfully like the cry of an abandoned baby.

"Well, laddie, them green berets have been in and out of here nearly every day that dawns of night on a week now. Dog-tired and their boots covered with clay from cliff climbing when they come back. Then it's straight into the 'Mucky Duck'" – he meant the dockside pub the Black Swan – "go sup the four-ale bar friggin' near dry when they get there." He took one last grateful draw at his Black Market cigarette before adding, with an air of finality, "Mark my words, son, there's something in the air—" He stopped short.

Three dark, lithe shapes were hurtling in at mast height, barely skimming the waves, their props beating the water into a white fury, cannon already chattering lethally. "Christ, how right I was, there is summat in the friggin' air!" the old dockie gasped and dropped to the oil-stained, wet jetty. "Tip-and-run raiders from France!"

Now the German Focke-Wulf fighter-bombers were directly overhead, their engines snarling in angry protest as the *Luftwaffe* pilots flung them into tight turns, their 20mm cannon barking all the while. They couldn't miss, for the harbour was packed with Allied shipping.

Masts snapped like matchwood, radio aerials came tumbling down in a crackle of furious blue-and-red sparks. One of the freighters, struck admidships, started to sink. Another, its desk packed with drums of diesel fuel, began to burn furiously. In an instant all was chaos and sudden, violent death.

"Frig this for a friggin' game o' sodgers!" the old dockie gasped. "I'm doin' a bunk!" He looked at the other man's scarred faced, as if he expected a reaction. There was none. "Ta, ta, then!" he growled over the vicious chatter of the planes' cannon and he was off.

Hard Man wasn't frightened. Indeed he felt it was his duty to stick it out at the docks, despite the danger. Something important might happen, just as he had learned something new about the commandos. It would all go in his report to *Marinenachrichten** in due course.

Now another battered fighter was blazing merrily. Panicking men were dropping over the sides, some already ringed in greedy blue flame, their hands beginning to burn and turn into charred claws as they attempted in vain to beat out that all-consuming fire.

Hard Man could feel the intense searing heat on his taut face. He gasped like an asthmatic in the throes of an attack as the very air was drawn from his lungs. But he didn't make a run for it. There would still be time to do

* German Naval Intelligence.

that. Even after months in the cage, he was tremendously fit; he'd make it.

Once more the pilots brought their planes round in a tight turn, trailing white exhaust smoke behind them, their engines shrieking with protest at the strain. Their pilots seemed to ignore the flak streaming up at them now, mixed with a terrific barrage of bullets from 'chicago pianos', massed batteries of .5-in machine-guns. They flew through a sky peppered almost solid with lethal shot. In the front, the flight leader zoomed in at sea level, risking striking the water only metres below, heading straight for the softest target in the packed harbour.

Hard Man, a person not given to admiration, whistled softly at the unknown pilot's daring. He seemed to bear a charmed life as he defied death at the hands of the Tommy gunners. They concentrated all their fire upon the lone aircraft, trying to cone the plane in. To no avail. Weaving and slipping from side to side in a masterly manner, the German pilot survived all their efforts to knock him out of the sky. Time and again he missed death by metres as the Focke-Wulf was rocked from side to side by yet another burst of angry, cherry-red flame close by.

Once the fighter-bomber disappeared completely in a cloud of thick grey smoke, slammed upwards as if punched by some giant invisible fist. Hard Man groaned. The unknown pilot had 'bought the farm', as the *Luftwaffe* men said. But he hadn't. Moments later he emerged from the cloud and zoomed down even lower still, heading straight for the flotilla of awkward-looking barges.

The commandos knew what to expect. Some dived rapidly overboard, the area around thrashed and peppered by the plane's shells. Others manned the barges' machine-guns and blazed away at the aircraft as it grew larger and larger in their sights. Still the German pilot pressed home his daring attack.

Not for long. Again the Focke-Wulf was struck as if by a giant flaming fist. Smoke started to pour from its ruptured engine. *"Keep going!"* Hard Man yelled exuberantly. "Hit the Tommy bastard . . . *keep going!"*

The unknown pilot did, although he was losing power by the instant. On the decks of the barges, the commandos armed with tommy-guns, legs straddled to keep their balance, blazed away at the plane like gun-slingers in a Hollywood western.

Suddenly the attacking plane staggered alarmingly. Had it been hit? Hard Man cried to himself. It hadn't. The next moment ugly black bombs started to tumble from the Focke-Wulf, turning and twisting as they followed their inevitable course towards the defenceless barges.

The sea heaved and spat. Great mushrooms of angry white water rushed upwards, at times obscuring the barges, which swung from side to side under the impact, threatening to capsize at any moment. Madly the commandos, dropping their now useless weapons, grabbed for handholds. Others crumpled to the soaked decks like bundles of wet rags.

Suddenly, one of the barges was hit mortally. Its blunt prow reared up into the air like a wild horse being put to the saddle for the first time. Almost instantly, it started to sink rapidly, tossing the gasping, shouting commandos into the boiling sea. Another barge was hit and it, too, started to sink.

But the steam was beginning to go out of the German surprise attack. Already, the Focke-Wulf pilots calculated, the Tommy fighters all along that highly vulnerable coast would be scrambling, aiming at bouncing the fighter-bombers before they could reach the shelter of their defences on the other side of the Channel. It was time to break off the attack and flee.

The damaged plane in the lead waggled its wings. It was the signal. In a tight curve, the Focke-Wulfs wheeled towards the east. At wavetop height, the fighter-bombers started to fly back the way they had come, keeping as low as they dared in order to avoid the Tommy radar screen.

Hard Man watched them go, as the sirens started to sound the 'All Clear' in the port, the continuous wail being taken up by siren after siren, getting louder as they approached the ravaged port. Hard Man took his eyes off the jetty, wondering if anyone had noticed him still standing there when he should have been in the shelters. No one had.

He turned his attention to the anchorage, the filthy, oil-stained water now littered with the pathetic bits and pieces floating on its surface from the battered and sunken ships. A lone figure had detached itself from the circle of corpses bobbing up and down around the sinking commando barge. With infinite slowness the Tommy was half-paddling, half-swimming towards the shore. Hard Man frowned. Should he let the survivor go under to his death. A moment later he decided against it. It wouldn't look good among the dockers, and he didn't want to draw any unwelcome attention to himself. His mind made up, he hurried down to the edge of the jetty to help the obviously grievously wounded commando.

Chapter Two

The commando was dying. Hard Man didn't need a doctor to tell him that. He had seen enough dying men in the past few years to know the signs. A burst of 20mm cannon shells had ripped his guts apart. Now his intestines lay pulsating on the oil-slick jetty, steaming slightly in the January cold.

The commando moaned softly. It didn't move Hard Man. He noted, however, the think pink blood trickling from the side of the Tommy's slack and gaping mouth. His nose was pinched and ashen. They were the signs of impending death.

Farther up the jetty the sweating, cursing men of the AFS in their black, thigh-high waders were trying to put out yet another fire. They were everywhere, the man kneeling next to the commando saw happily. Serve the Tommies right, he told himself, still angry at the way he was always called a 'Hun'.

Coming ever closer was the urgent jingle of the bell of an ambulance approaching at speed. Hard Man knew it was already too late. The commando would be dead by the time it arrived. He had only minutes to live, he guessed. Still, he told himself, he might get something useful from the dying Tommy, something that he could pass on to the people in Naval Intelligence when he got back to the Reich.

"Help coming soon," he said without feeling as the dying man took hold of his hand weakly, as if he felt he needed reassurance.

"Ta," the Tommy gasped. "Ta, mate." The man looked up at Hard Man. With his ugly face he didn't look a day over 20. It didn't matter to Hard Man. In the last terrible years he had seen even younger men die in combat. "I've had it mate . . . gonna turn me toes up."

Hard Man didn't attempt to persuade him that he wasn't. What did a dying Tommy mean to him? It was one fewer of the bastards to shoot or put away in the camps after Churchill had surrendered to the Führer.

The commando forced a tortured grin. "By heck, I couldn't half go a last pint o' wallop with the lads!" The remark made him cough thickly. Blood trickled from his slack lips once more.

With the edge of his sleeve, Hard Man wiped it away. There was no feeling in his gesture. It was just something one did.

"Suppose I won't be going to that Frog port with 'em now. The CO said it was going to be a wizard show. It'd be in all the papers – even Part Two Orders," he meant the *News of the World*, "Pity."

"What Frog port?"

The commando tried to answer and give him the name, but failed lamentably. He shook his head in weak anger. "Can't get me tongue round the place's name . . . Saint . . ." Again he tried and failed. "They sez old Winnie has personally ordered the attack."

Hard Man's dark cruel eyes lit up at the mention of 'attack'. "What did you say?" he demanded sharply. "Attack on this – er – Frog port?"

The commando nodded numbly.

11

Hard Man was tempted to shake the dying man in order to make him speak, but decided against it. One of the dockers might be watching and that wouldn't look good, once the civvies realised who he was. "I say, can—"

He never finished his urgent question. A heavy hand fell on his right shoulder, hard.

Hard Man looked up startled. A tall, hard-faced military policeman, eyes stern and suspicious underneath his red cap, was staring down at him, other hand poised on his leather pistol holster. "I'm looking after the poor chap," he stuttered, caught by surprise. "Poor geezer," he used the colloquial word to detract from his accent, "He's a goner."

The Redcap wasn't impressed, "You're a Hun prisoner of war, ain't yer?" he barked. "What yer doing poking yer nose into what's going on here, eh?"

Hard Man didn't have an answer and the Redcap went on to say, "This could mean the cooler for you, Jerry. You're off back to the camp before yer friggin' plates o' meat can touch the friggin' ground!"

Hard Man forgot the dying commando and the raid he had mentioned. "*Arschloch*" he cursed in his native language.

The Redcap tightened his hold on the German's muscular bicep. "None of yer friggin' Hun lip to me!" he threatened, "or it'll be the worse for yer. Now are yer gonna come quietly? Or have I got to cuff yer, eh?"

Tamely Hard Man surrendered, lowering his head so that the policeman could not see the red rage that blazed in his dark eyes. "Yes, you'll have no trouble with me."

The cop laughed grimly. "Oh, pity!" he said. "I wouldn't have minded getting yer down the cells and giving yer a little bit o' what for, after this." He indicated the dead commando. "All right, move it."

Hard Man moved it. Behind him the commando died quietly, stiffening unnoticed on the jetty in a crimson star of his own blood.

Captain Harkins took his time. He knocked the dottle out of his pipe bowl into the overflowing ashtray, watched by Hard Man and a cautious middle-aged staff sergeant who only too well knew Hard Man's reputation for sudden violence. He had been at the receiving end of it twice already. He looked from the prisoner to Captain Harkins MC and his look said, 'Dangerous and bloody bolshy, sir.'

Harkins, middle-aged and a little overweight after 20 years as a solicitor between the two wars, didn't seem to notice. But he understood the grizzled NCO's feelings. His was the attitude taken by most of the inmates, staff and prisoners, at the POW camp. Even the German 'Blacks',* the hard-core POWs, disliked him.

As the *Lageralteste*† *Kapitanleutnant* Duvendag had often remarked to Harkins, the camp's Intelligence Officer, *"Ein arrogantes Schwein, Herr Hauptmann,* thinks only of himself. I don't really trust him, you know. Typical U-boat officer. Think they are winning the war by themselves. Have no time for lowly stubble-hoppers and surface men like myself."

---

* In WWII, German POWs were divided into three categories: 'Blacks', dyed-in-the wool Nazis; 'Whites', anti-Nazis; and the great majority, 'Greys', who had been fellow-travellers. 'Warm' indicated homosexual.
† Senior POW and liaison man between the prisoners and their jailers.

Now Harkins dismissed the apprehensive NCO with "All right, staff, go and get yourself a cup of cocoa in the cookhouse."

The noncom looked at the middle-aged ex-infantry officer who had won his Military Cross in the trenches in the Old War – some said it should have been the Victoria Cross for such outstanding bravery – and hesitated.

Harkins smiled winningly and indicated once again that he should go. Reluctantly he did so. Now, Harkins went through the slow routine of refilling his pipe from the old leather pouch, taking his time, lighting several matches and puffing away until apparently he was satisfied that the plug tobacco he favoured was well and truly alight.

In the old days as a country solicitor that routine had impressed some village yokel who had been naughty. It had put his nerves on edge. But not Hard Man. He stared at the old Englishman contemptuously, as if to say: 'What kind of fool do you take me for, Mister Captain? Those methods don't frighten an old hare like myself.'

In the end Harkins gave up and said in his excellent German, learned in the old Imperial German POW Camp at Holzminden: "Sit down. There are cigarettes in the silver box. Help yourself if you wish."

Hard Man was not going to be bribed either. "*Nein Danke, Herr Hauptmann*," he said coldly.

Harkins shrugged. "Have it your way," he muttered, after casting a quick glance at Hard Man's POW record, which was pretty long for a man who was supposed to be confined to a rural camp some square mile in area.

"This is the second time you have changed uniform with a common soldier to get out of the camp," he commenced. "What—"

"*Hun*," Hard Man interrupted him firmly. "Your people

14

keep calling us Germans, Huns. But we Germans are not Huns. They came from the East somewhere – fat, squat, yellow people." He pointed through the window at his fellow POWs wearily tramping the circuit, round and round the earthen compound of the cage, watched by the wary guards in their stork-legged wooden towers. "Do they look yellow and squat to you, *Herr Hauptmann?*" he demanded.

Harkins ignored the outburst, though it was strange for Hard Man to reveal his emotions. Perhaps he had the tough-looking German U-boat officer rattled at last. He hoped so. He was sick of the man's tricks. "You know that officers are not supposed to work while prisoners under the terms of the Geneva Convention," he pointed out quietly.

Hard Man contained himself. There was too much at stake for him to lose his temper, especially now when he felt he was onto something, though he didn't know exactly what. Yet that dead commando meant something. "I'm just bored with being inside the cage all the time," he answered. "Same faces, same places, same conversations. All that classy talk about German *Kultur* some of those land-lubber officers indulge in." He could not resist the sneer at those of his fellow officers who killed the time with poetry readings, needlework and the like. "Besides I want something *physical*. I need to use my muscles instead of my head all the time, *Herr Hauptmann.*"

"We could put you down the saltmines as your chaps did to ours in the last show," Harkins ventured mildly.

But as usual irony was wasted on Hard Man.

Harkins stared at him in that bored, cynical manner of his which he often affected in his interrogations of hard-nosed POWs, as if he didn't believe a single word they said. "I thought you'd done enough things physical," he said after a while." He glanced again at the POW's record. "Spanish Civil War. Helped to sink the Republican cruiser *El Pveblo* in '37. Action against the Polish Navy trapped in the Baltic in '39. Twenty-thousand tons of shipping reportedly sunk . . . The *Royal Oak* affair in Scapa Flow. Over a thousand of our poor lads sent to a watery grave. Isn't that physical enough for you, *Herr Leutnant?*"

Hard Man shrugged. "That was different."

Harkins gave up on him. Indeed he was momentarily tempted to strike out at the prisoner with his ashplant. He swiftly fought off the urge. "All right," he said with an air of dismissal. "Fourteen days in the cooler." He raised his voice so that the NCO outside the door could hear. "Staff, wheel the prisoner away. Fourteen days in the cooler. Enter it in the book."

"*Danke, Herr Hauptmann,*" Hard Man said with a smirk and gave a little bow from the waist.

Harkins ignored the gesture. Hard Man would have to get up earlier in the day to take the rise out of him.

Five minutes later Hard Man, escorted by two middle-aged guards, bayonets fixed, was plodding across the compound towards the cells at the far end.

Under normal circumstances, his fellow POWs would have stopped walking the circuit to make ribald remarks, boo the guards, perhaps even cheer their fellow prisoner for his audacity. Not now. Nobody liked or trusted Hard Man. They watched him being led to the cooler in silence, if they watched at all. Even his fellow naval officers, 'Blacks' to the man, remained silent and sullen.

Hard Man smiled. What did he care? Let them play their silly games. He knew that a handful of the bolder

16

'Blacks' were currently digging a tunnel. Some of them doing the circuit were indeed getting rid of the earth from the tunnel beneath one of the cookhouse stoves, emptying it from sacks concealed inside their trouser legs opened by strings leading from their pockets. They were doomed to failure. Sooner or later that clever swine Captain Harkins would get onto them. He always did. All the same, he was glad the fools were working on the tunnel. In due course he would use its presence for his own purposes. Moments later he was stood to attention as the Tommy lance-corporal fumbled with the key to the cooler, snarling, "Bread and water for you m'lad. Perhaps that'll knock some o' the piss and vinegar out of yer."

Hard Man didn't respond. When did a German U-boat officer comment on the ramblings of a has-been Tommy lance-corporal?

From his office window, puffing reflectively at his old briar pipe, which had given him so much comfort in the trenches in the last show, Harkins watched the little scene. He sighed like a man sorely tried. Hard Man was up to something. Why else these two attempts at getting out of the POW camp? He knew that in his bones. *But what?*

In the three years since the first enemy prisoners had been arriving in the UK to be shipped off to the POW cages, not *one* German had managed to escape. After all, the country was an island. Now, in 1942, security was even tighter. Hard Man didn't stand in a chance in hell, he told himself. All the same . . . He left the rest of that unpleasant thought unsaid. He glanced at his watch. It was nearly time to go to the pub where Mabel, his wife, would be waiting for him in the bar. They had managed to secure two rooms in that run-down place. It was against

17

orders for an officer to bring his wife to his place of duty, but who concerned himself with orders? He had learned to disregard them back in 1915 when he had first gone into the line in France.

He rose and limped over to the hat-stand, his wooden leg squeaking audibly as he did so. He took his battered cap and placed it squarely on his greying head. He needed a drink urgently, even at black market prices.

He gave Hard Man once last thought and then dismissed him for that day with a muttered, "Bloody bastard! *God-dam the Huns . . .*"

Chapter Three

Naval officers were rare at the Führer's HQ at Rastenburg. It was well known that the Leader disliked the sea and everything that sailed on it. His last visit to his new navy had been in the late 1930s when he had gone to visit the newest German pocket battleship, the *Deutschland* at Hamburg. For a start, the port city was a place he hated anyway. It was full of communists and left-wingers. Apart from the cheers from the Hitler Youth and the SA organised by the local 'golden pheasants',* he had been greeted in Hamburg by a stoney silence. His mood had not been improved by the short voyage he had taken on the new, gleaming, powerful battleship. That had ended with his being violently sick. He had returned to Berlin in an angry huff. Since then he had never visited his *Kriegsmarine*.

Accordingly, the high-ranking delegation of naval officers received curious stares as they left their fleet of grey-painted Mercedes and headed for the wooden operations room hidden in the firs, followed by elegant aides lugging the heavy leather briefcases filled to overflowing with maps, charts, notes and so on which the naval officers

* Party officials, known thus on account of their splendid colourful uniforms, adorned with a great deal of gold braid.

would use in the all-important briefing this cold winter's morning.

For once the Führer was on time. Indeed he was waiting for the naval delegation, stroking his Alsation bitch Blondi and popping yet another of the 60 pills prescribed daily for him by his quack.

For a moment or two, Admiral Otto Ciliax, tall, plump and silver-haired, in charge of the naval officers, was worried. Was he late? No one was ever late for a Führer briefing. If he was, he was never asked again. That meant the Russian front and final obscurity.

But his worries were unnecessary. The Führer advanced upon him, face wreathed in smiles, both hands extended to take those of the surprised Admiral's. "How awfully good of you to come, *Her Admiral!*" he gushed warmly. "I hope the journey from France wasn't too tiresome," he added in his thick Austrian accent and farted at the same time, the result of the many gas pills he swallowed daily.

Ciliax blanched with the awful smell and Blondi darted behind the table, wimpering softly, tail between its legs. Hitler, for his part, didn't seem to notice.

He let go of the nauseated sailor's hand and said, "Now then, *mein lieber Admiral*, what have you got to tell me about our capital ships?"

Hastily, trying to forget the overpowering stench from the Führer's bowels, caused by the vegetarian diet he took to keep him slim and the laxatives he needed because of it to move his innards, Ciliax signalled to the elegant aides with their gold lanyards and shining dirks. Immediately they started to unpack their papers, the results of many weeks of research off the French coast and into the Channel.

In the meantime he commenced his exposé, detailing

his plans which he had learned by heart for this all-important meeting; the documentation would come later. "The *Scharnhorst* and *Gneisenau*, both 32,000 tons in displacement, have been in Brest harbour since last March. As you know, *mein* Führer, both had a very successful fighting cruise in the North Atlantic before then."

"Yes," Hitler said, then surprised the silver-haired Admiral, "They sank twenty-two Allied merchant ships, totalling 115,600 tons." He beamed at the sailor, pleased at the effect he had created among the naval officers. He, too, had come prepared and he wanted them to know it. "Since then they have lunguished in port uselessly – two warships which can outrun and outgun anything the English possess."

"*Jawohl, mein* Führer," Ciliax said a little uneasily. He hadn't expected Hitler to know such details. "Naturally, since last March, Churchill has used all his air strength in an attempt to knock them out. He—"

"Without success," Hitler interrupted him firmly letting rip another tremendous fart. The room was flooded again with the noxious gas and under the table Blondi howled piteously, as if it couldn't stand much more. Hitler, as usual, did not seem to notice. "However, Herr Churchill may well succeed in starving the two capital ships into inactivity. The bombing is stopping most of their supplies reaching them. We have the figures somewhere or other."

"Yes, of course," Ciliax agreed uneasily, "But we have succeeded in keeping them at the ready with the most vital supplies needed for a short battle cruise."

Hitler smiled winningly at the flustered Admiral. "Now that's the kind of talk I like to hear, my dear Ciliax. Pray continue."

Once again, Ciliax cleared his throat, encouraged by Hitler's attitude. It was rare that he had anything positive to remark about the German Navy's surface ships. Whatever praise he had for the *Kriegsmarine* was usually reserved for that fanatic Doenitz's U-boat Army.

"The time has come, *mein* Führer," he announced proudly, "for the *Gneisenau* and *Scharnhorst* to make a break for it. Show the Tommies that we are not impotent, can only dance to their tune."

"*Excellent . . . excellent!*" Hitler chortled happily, raising his right leg in that characteristic gesture of his when he was pleased. Blondi thought the movement signified something else. Beneath the table the big dog tensed expectantly, tail between its legs, ready to flee the room altogether if that awful small occurred again in the next few moments. For his part, Admiral Ciliax looked a little apprehensive as well. Like all sailors he had a very sensitive stomach. It was easily upset at the best of times.

But both the dog and the Admiral were mistaken on this occasion. Hitler stamped down his booted foot happily, without breaking wind as they feared, saying, "Now then, Admiral, what is your plan?"

Ciliax launched immediately into the details of the great breakout which he and his staff officers had been planning for several weeks now, ignoring the RAF planes which had bombed the port of Brest day after day. His exposé was interrupted at regular intervals by the ensigns pushing charts and maps in front of him so that he could explain more thoroughly to an attentive Führer. And for once Adolf Hitler did not interrupt with one of his long-winded and often irrelevant harangues.

But when Ciliax, a little red-faced and worn, ended,

Hitler obviously felt it was his duty as the Supreme Commander of the Armed Forces of Greater Germany to sum up. As a weary Ciliax said afterwards to his cronies, gratefully sipping at a very large French cognac, "He always has to give his mustard to any plan. Still, he bought it this time."

Hitler certainly had. He said, "From past experience I don't believe the Tommies are capable of making and carrying out lightning decisions as we Germans can. Perhaps it is all that dreadful China tea with warm milk that they drink." He allowed himself a smile at what he took for a joke. Dutifully they responded in kind. "It is my belief that they will be incapable of transferring their bomber and fighter aircraft to south-east England for an attack on our ships when they pass through the narrows of the Dover Straits. The speed which you predict for your capital ships, my dear Admiral Ciliax, will make that impossible for them."

There was a murmur of agreement from the assembled naval staff officers.

The Führer sighed a little as if everything was a great effort. "Picture, if you would," he continued all the same, "what would happen if the situation were reversed and a surprise report came in that two British battleships had appeared in the Thames Estuary and were heading for the Dover Straits. Even *we*, as efficient as we German always are, would be scarcely able to bring up our aircraft swiftly and methodically."

Suddenly Hitler's voice rose. It was filled abruptly with that thick Austrian fervour which once had roused the brown-shirted mob to a frenzy at the annual Party rally at Nuremburg before the war. "I agree with you, *Herr Admiral*, there is nothing to be gained by leaving our capital ships at Brest, however safe they may be behind concrete and steel there. Their flypaper effect, as I call it, of tying up the Tommy's air force there, may not last much longer. They'll find other means of attacking the *Gneisenau* and *Scharnhorst*, I am sure sabotage, midget submarines and the like. Only as long as our battleships remain battleworthy will the enemy feel obliged to attack." He raised his forefinger as if in warning. "But the moment the two of them are seriously damaged the Tommies will discontinue their attack and leave them to wither on the vine."

Hitler stared sternly at Ciliax in that 'man of destiny' pose which he affected on such occasions and rasped, "*Herr Admiral*, on the eleventh of February – I have checked the weather charts and the tides personally – you will take the *Gneisenau* and *Scharnhorst* out of Brest and proceed at full speed – do not concern yourself about the fuel, it can be replaced – up the English Channel. Your objective will be in north Germany, Kiel to be exact. Clear?"

"*Klar, mein* Führer!" Ciliax snapped back, face and body rigid as he thought of what lay before his beloved battleships.

"Good," Hitler smiled, master of the situation as usual, especially when his subordinates didn't object to his plans, however wild and risky. "And let me tell you this: I would be willing to pay a thousand gold Reichsmarks personally to see the look on that drunken Jewish sot's face,"—he meant Churchill's – "when he learns just how we have tricked him at Brest and humbled what is still the greatest sea power in the world." Carried away by his own enthusiasm, Hitler could not contain himself any longer, not that he concerned himself with such trivial matters;

after all he *was* master of the whole of Europe from the Channel to the Caucasus. He broke wind, loudly.

Blondi howled and bolted for the door. Moments later Admiral Ciliax and his staff officers left equally speedily, trying to keep their mouths shut and hardly daring to breathe until they were outside in the cold, clean winter air of the headquarters.

"Well," Ciliax said with an air of finality as they waited for their cars to arrive from the motor pool, watched keenly by the gigantic SS men of Hitler's bodyguard, "I think we shall pull it off. The element of surprise the Führer emphasised should do the trick."

Behind him one of the young ensigns, peaked cap tilted at a jaunty angle on his well-trimmed hair, whispered to his companion, another young ensign, "Yes, we'll pull it off. But Lord have mercy on those we leave behind in France. Churchill's going to exact a terrible revenge for having his nose rubbed in the shit in his own backyard."

"Amen to that, Heinz," the other young officer whispered. Then the Mercedes arrived to take them away, leaving behind a hesitant Blondi hiding in the firs, as if the bitch was wondering whether it would ever come out again to face that terrible barrage of high-class farts.

Chapter Four

Just after dawn had risen, the flotilla of German E-boats came hissing across the dark-green sea from Cherbourg. They seemed to skim above the surface of the water as two white trails of crazy white spray spurted up behind them like wings. As the petty officer signalled the course with his flags, they careened round in a great circle, splitting into two formations and taking up their guard positions on the far side of the inner screen of destroyers. The force was ready for anything.

Admiral Ciliax nodded his silent approval. Everything was going according to plan. Now his escape force totalled 25 ships, and already on the horizon to the east he could see the dark moving spots which were his air cover arriving from their French fields. The great gamble was going to pay off, just as the Führer had said it would.

The Admiral turned to his second in command of the *Scharnhorst*. "When the fighters arrive," he commanded, "signal them to fly just above the water. I don't want the Tommy radar to pick them up at this stage of the op."

"*Jawohl, Herr Admiral*," the Commander said dutifully. He turned to the waiting signaller. "Bunts." he ordered, "break cover. Stand by to send message." The fleet had been on radio and general silence for six hours. Now the petty officer was glad of the movement. He tensed behind his signal lamp.

Another hour passed . . . and another in anxious, tense expectation. The fleet encountered a new and uncharted enemy minefield off Dieppe. Hurriedly four minesweepers, the old-fashioned, coal-burning type, were ordered up to do a quick sweep. Ciliax, very nervous and sweating now despite the bone-freezing cold, took a chance. He ordered the two capital ship to pass through the hastily swept channel. He was going to risk a mine floating there with deadly intent. They did so. Nothing happened. Their luck was still holding out. He murmured a quick prayer of relief . . .

At eleven o'clock precisely, a young signals lieutenant clattered up to the bridge. He started to blurt out something. Ciliax, the old school naval officer, didn't give him a chance to do so. "First, salute!" he commanded.

The boy flushed. Obediently he saluted.

"Well?"

"Intercept, *Herr Admiral.*" The young officer thrust the message at the senior officer as if it were red-hot.

"*Damned shit!*" Ciliax cursed when he had read it.

"What is it?" his second in command asked anxiously.

"The Tommies have got wind of us. Fighters, capital ships and twenty other smaller craft, all steaming full out for the Straits of Dover."

"Heaven, arse and cloudburst!" the Commander cursed, "Now the tick-tock is really in the pisspot!"

Ciliax ignored the bad language. He was too worried to note it even. Now the secret was out. He had a fight on his hands . . .

*   *   *

27

The twin-engined Wellington bombers, the Fleet Air Arm's Swordfish – 'stringbags', the Royal Navy called them contemptuously – supported by Spitfires, attacked time and time again. They did so without plan.

The German Focke-Wulfs and Messerschmitts, on the other hand, had every tactical move planned in advance.

The German fighters came winging in parallel to the enemy attack force. They zoomed upwards as if on an express lift. At 400 kilometres an hour, yellow engine nose spinners whirling, they hit the English slow squadrons, while the others kept climbing to attack the Tommies above.

Wellingtons began to fall out of the grey, overcast sky like metal leaves. Great pieces of fabric dropped off them as they were torn to shreds by the German cannon fire. Parachutes streamed into the atmosphere. Here and there one of two opened, but the altitude was too low for the rest. They plummeted down to the sea to hit it with a terrible splash.

The Focke-Wulfs lowered their undercarriages as one. It was all planned. Their speed fell at once. Now they started to fire merciless deflection shots. At that slow speed and at that range they couldn't miss.

The fighters hissed above the shattered British squadrons. Their pilots cursed angrily as ice began to form on their canopies at that height. It blinded them. Still they set about their pre-arranged mission, hoping that it would work now that they were fighting blind.

They released the numbers of little parachute bombs beneath their wings. It was a new aerial weapon and a new tactic, but it worked splendidly in spite of the ice. Almost immediately the small sticks started to explode among the twin-engined British Wellington bombers and the effect was devasting. The British pilots had no idea of what had hit them until it was too late. The first Wellington was hit. It disintegrated in a burst of cherry-red, angry flame and smoke engulfed it. Then there was nothing but a shower of debris falling to the sea far below and what looked like an abandoned football hurtling through the sky, the severed head of the pilot, complete with leather flying helmet.

Another bomber was struck. Its port wing crumpled under the impact and the Wellington slipped to one side, streaming out of the sky, engines shrieking, trailing thick black smoke behind it. It smacked into the sea and sank at once. A great white whirling mushroom of angry water shot upwards.

More and more of the bombers followed. The smoke-speckled sky was full of crippled and dying bombers. Everywhere aircrew were baling out, chancing the machine-guns of trigger-happy German fighter pilots, carried away by the savage bloodlust of combat. All was confusion and lethal chaos.

Still the British pressed home their attack doggedly. With a kind of helpless fatalism, just as the dark smudge of the Belgian coast came into view, bringing with it fresh German fighter planes from their fields around Brussels, the 'Stringbags' entered the fray. Cumbersome, flying at half the speed of the slowest German fighter; the Swordfish biplanes – they had been obsolete ten years before – started to drop mines in the path of the German fleet. Almost immediately the German ships took up the challenge. Their 88mm cannon thundered. Twin-barrelled 20mm Oerlikon quick-firers pumped away furiously, throwing a thousand rounds of glowing white shells skywards every minute. It was as if the 'Stringbags' were ploughing straight into a solid wall.

But the brave efforts of the doomed Fleet Air Arm pilots

was not for nought. Suddenly, Admiral Ciliax's flagship *Scharnhorst* was shaken by a tremendous explosion. The whole mighty superstructure trembled. Masts came tumbling down. A lifeboat broke loose and went slithering over the side. The deck trembled like a live thing. Sailors lost their grip. Hastily others grabbed for holds.

On the bridge, the deck momentarily obscured by smoke below, Admiral Ciliax cursed mightily as the *Scharnhorst* started to slow down. He yelled for the radio officer to report, but then the harassed young lieutenant appeared personally to cry, "Radios out, *Herr Admiral.* Take them a while to come back, sir."

"*Verdammte Scheisse,*" Ciliax cursed. Radios going now. He knew he couldn't command the fleet without radio contact with his other ships. He made his decision hastily as the *Scharnhorst*, trailing an oily wake behind her, slowed down even more. He hated to do so, but this was no time to stick to the antiquated naval doctrine of a captain going down with his ship. Besides, he had 25 other ships under his command.

"*Los,*" he cried above the crack and snap of the anti-aircraft fire, "Number One, whistle up the destroyer *Z-29.* I'll transfer my command to her for the time being. She can take me and my command staff off.'

"Ay, ay, sir," the Commander bellowed back obediently.

While he waited, Admiral Ciliax stared at the sky. The weather was beginning to deteriorate rapidly. Visibility was down to two kilometres. Cloud ceiling couldn't be more than 200 metres. Any minute, he knew from experience, it would start to rain. The weather was in their favour now. Under the cover of the bad weather, the captain of the stricken *Scharnhorst* might be able to get the battleship underway once more. The *Scharnhorst* was a tough bird. She could stand a lot of punishment and with a bit of luck he would do so before the Tommies launched an all-out attack on this now tempting target.

Five minutes later Admiral Ciliax was being winched across the heaving green sea in a bosun's chair. Behind him he left the stricken battleship to her fate.

"Object ahead!" the destroyer's Number One sang out.

"Straight ahead. Four miles."

Immediately the young officers on the bridge, huddled in their duffel coats, caps tilted at the rakish angles affected by destroyer officers, raised their glasses.

A great grey shape slid silently into the circles of bright, calibrated glass. "Christ Almighty," the Number One cried, recognising the ship immediately from the identification tables they pored over daily in the wardroom, "the bloody *Scharnhorst!*"

"You're right, Number One!" the Captain agreed excitedly, bracing his feet against the wildly heaving deck as the destroyer gathered speed. "All 32,000 tons of her and nine-inch guns."

"Oh, my aching back!" Number One gave a mock moan. "What good are our five-inch popguns against that kind of artillery?"

"We'll soon find out!"

"You're going in to attack?"

"You bet your life I am, Number One!" the Captain snapped. He forced a tight smile. "Think of all those luscious popsies we'll able to bed on the strength of this."

"What a fighting motto. 'Fight and fuck for England and St George'."

"Something like that," the young skipper agreed and

then concentrated on his attack as the distance between David and Goliath diminished rapidly.

On the open bridge, ignoring the drenching spray, the officers watched intently as the *Scharnhorst* loomed ever larger. The young skipper whistled down the voice-tube as the last of the ancient 'Stringbags' fell out of the grey-peppered sky, trailing flame behind it as it dived to its death. "Stand by forrard tubes," he commanded.

The obedient answer of the chief torpedo mate came back in muffled excitement.

Now the skipper felt that the last of the steam had started to leave the British attack as the first drops of rain began to patter down. It looked as if it was up to him to notch up some success to rescue the honour of the Royal Navy.

"Torpedoes, closed in," his Number One yelled above the tremendous thunder of the German big guns.

Crazily the little destroyer heeled from side to side, her masts almost touching the water several times, as the shells plummeted down close by. The young skipper ignored the danger, his unlined face set and determined as he ran in for the vital attack. It was now or never, he told himself. "Stand by to fire one—" he began.

His words were drowned by the screech of a great shell tearing the sky apart like canvas being ripped in two. The deck rose up to meet him. "What the hell is going on?" he cried in sudden alarm. Next instant a steel plate slammed into his face and his nose broke at once. Thick red blood arced from his shattered nostrils. He tried and failed to keep upright. Feeling sick and giddy he went down on his knees, fighting gamely not to black out, like a stricken boxer refusing to go down for a count of ten. He didn't make it. A black veil descended upon him and he fell face down in a mess of his own blood and knew no more.

Number One, cap vanished, bleeding from a jagged cut in his forehead, completed the order. "Fire one!"

The hurrying destroyer shivered violently. There was a wild flurry of bubbles at her bow. A deadly grey shape zipped across the surface and then vanished.

"Count running time," Number One heard himself order. But the bridge was packed with dead and dying, a confusion of shattered, bloody limbs. There was no one to check the torpedo. Blindly he fumbled for his own watch. He started to count off the seconds, his voice getting weaker by the instant. "*Sixty . . . forty-five . . . thirty . . .*!" Abruptly the stopwatch tumbled from his nerveless fingers. Blindly, he bent to retrieve it.

Suddenly, as the destroyer now without a single officer on his feet, hurtled leaderless towards the great battleship, her guns ceased firing.

On the battle-littered deck, trying to fight their way to the shattered bridge through the tangle of wires and twisted steel girders, the ratings, urged on by their petty officers, saw why.

A squadron of me 109s – nine of them – were hurtling through the drifting smoke straight at the destroyer. They came in line abreast, machine-guns and cannons already singing their song of death. The rescuers ducked for cover. They knew it was no use now attempting to rescue the bridge. All of them, bridge and deck, were doomed.

A moment later the shells swamped the little destroyer in lethal fury. They ripped up the deck. Glass splintered. The last of the radio masts came clattering down in a frenzy of furious sparks. Smoke poured from the shattered hatches. Men went down everywhere, clutching their mutilated bodies, chests ripped apart, drowning and gurgling in their own life blood.

A wounded, lone petty officer attempted to take charge. He fought his way to the bridge and stepped over the bodies of the dead and dying. He whistled down the voice tube in the same instant that his chest was shattered by a glowing-white cannon shell. Somehow or other he managed to utter the last order! "Make smoke . . . engine room . . . for God's sake . . . *make smoke. . .*" Then he, too, fell to the deck, dead before he hit the blood-soaked planks.

But the engine room reacted. As the steering went and the dying destroyer started to steam round in aimless circles, thick white smoke began to pour from its twin stacks. The German fighters fired one last triumphant burst and then, their ammunition exhausted, they were turning to wing their way back to their bases, to the whores and the ice-cold champagne waiting for them there to celebrate the great victory.

Steadily, the German fleet sailed on into the North Sea, disappearing into the grey squalls of ice-cold, bitter rain. Hitler had succeeded. The German Navy had attempted and succeeded in defying the might of the greatest fleet in the world. For the first time in 300 years the English had been beaten on their own doorstep . . . and already frantic signals were winging their way back to the Empire's capital to inform the King-Emperor's Chief Minister of that great disgrace . . .

Chapter Five

"Doerr. . . . *Leutnant* Doerr."

The big ex-U-boat navigator turned, startled.

It was Hard Man standing at the entrance to his hut, hidden from the rest of the compound and the POWs pounding the circuit wearily by several lines of none-too-clean washing.

"What is it?" Doerr asked coldly. He and the other U-boat man hadn't exchanged a word for months. He was a 'Black' like Hard Man, but he didn't like – or trust – the latter one bit.

"Thought I'd give you a hand with the tunnel," Hard Man said coolly.

Doerr gasped and then pulled himself together swiftly. "What tunnel?" he barked.

"Oh, come off it. Everybody knows about it." The other man kept his gaze lowered so that Doerr couldn't see the look in his eyes.

Hastily the other man cast a look around the compound to check whether they were being watched. But no one was taking the slightest notice. Even the guards were bored. Hard Man smiled. The supposedly tough U-boat man, who had fought to remain a 'Black' despite the pressure that Harkins and the rest had put on him to change, was in reality a big, scared pussy cat.

35

"Why?" Doerr asked in a whisper, as if some Tommy was lurking just around the corner.

"Because I'm bored. I don't want to be included in the escape party. I haven't earned that privilege naturally. But I've plenty of muscle power." He flexed his right arm so that the other man could see the muscles ripple beneath the tight material of his shabby, dyed battledress. "I'm getting stale in this place."

"You worked on the tunnel before?" Doerr asked.

"Yes, it went from the parcel room." Hard Man meant the place where the senior German officer and a British officer examined the POWs' parcels from the Reich, ensuring that all foodstuffs in tins and jars, that might be stored and used for an escape, were cut open so that their contents had to be eaten immediately. "We were all Blacks," Hard Man continued. "But that Warm brother," – he meant homosexual – "Jansen had been turned. He spilled the beans to the Tommies when they promised him a cushy number with his own kind at that camp in Scotland."

"What happened?" Doerr asked, interested in spite of himself.

Hard Man grinned, but there was no warmth about it and his dark eyes shone as cruelly as ever. "Well, put it like this, Jansen never used the Vaseline again, if you follow what I mean."

Doerr gave an involuntary gasp. "You mean—"

"I do. We had to. He was an object lesson for the rest of the weak sisters, especially those 'Whites'. It showed that there was no escaping National Socialist justice even when held by the enemy." He let his words sink in and Doerr looked impressed.

"What did you do to him?"

36

"Can't you guess? We had to set an example, but we didn't want any trouble with the enemy. They had their tunnel, thanks to the pansy bastard, and that had to be an end to it as far as they were concerned. Jansen *had* to die and the rest had to know that, but not the Tommies."

"So?"

Hard Man give him a flash of his malicious eyes, and in spite of himself the other man shivered slightly at that dangerous look. "We killed him. Killed him in a way that everyone of the POWs would know we'd done it and one that would frighten the shit out of any other would-be traitor."

Doerr swallowed a little hesitantly. He wanted to know how, but at the same time he didn't. Still, in the end, his curiosity got the better of him and he asked, "What way?"

"We lured him to the thunderboxes with the help of Kraemer. He was before your time. He went to the bottom last December when one of our boats torpedoed the Tommy merchantman taking a bunch of our chaps to Canada. Pity". He shrugged carelessly and Doerr told himself that Hard Man didn't really care one shit about the drowned POWs. In all probability he was glad that the other man had gone to the bottom of the Atlantic. Dead men don't talk.

"We let him – Kraemer – make up. Used flour from the cookhouse as powder and red paint from the drama company as lipstick. Jansen thought he'd found the honey pot." Hard Man laughed harshly. "And in a way he had, only this honeydew pile was made of shit."

"How do you mean?"

"You'll see. So up trots Jansen, cock in his hand, thinking he was going to get a bit of the other in the thunderbox just before lights out. What a mistake he made! We were waiting for him. Young Kraemer did his disappearing act so that he had an alibi for later, and me and half a dozen of the other officers took over. He screamed, just like a friggin' female, when he saw that we had taken the lid of the big eight-seat crapper. I think he guessed what we were going to do. All of us were armed with broomsticks and the like, you see," he added, eyes as malicious as ever. "All of us were going to get involved, so that there'd be no backing out later if the Tommies started an enquiry. We were *all* to take part in the murder."

"*Murder?*" Doerr gasped, shocked.

Hard Man laughed drily. "What did you think was going to happen? We're inviting him to a tea party or something with *puffer** and herbal tea like a bunch of old female farts."

He let his words sink in for a moment before continuing. "Of course, he tried to pull back, but he didn't have a chance. We started whacking him hard. And believe you me all of them enjoyed it at that moment, whatever they said to the contrary later."

Doerr didn't respond to the statement and Hard Man let his mind wander back to that night: the victim fighting hysterically not to go under in that evil yellow slime; the men gasping and panting as if in the throes of sexual excitement as time and time again they struck him mercilessly and finally the victim giving up with a sigh of despair to disappear into the ordure, hands breaking the foul yellow surface for a moment until all that was left was his upturned face, gazing up at them, all panic vanished. Then he had gone altogether. All that

* A German potato-cake.

had been left – momentarily – had been the air bubbles popping and exploding for a few seconds more until they, too, had stopped and the killers were trailing back to the showers, shoulders bent like those of broken men, saying nothing.

Now, as Doerr listened in horrified fascination, Hard Man thought of that murder and the new tunnel, the first germ of an idea beginning to uncurl in his evil, fertile imagination.

"You know how these tunnels work," Doerr said finally, breaking the heavy silence, glad to change the subject.

Hard Man nodded. "Down the shaft with the trolley to the earth surface, empty milk tins – Canadian Klim dried milk cans are the best – attached to a pump to clear away the foul air. Big problems are finding wood to shore up the sides and, above all, getting rid of the soil." He looked hard at Doerr, "You mean I'm on?"

Doerr nodded slowly, wondering if he were doing the right thing.

"Good . . . thanks." He didn't reach out to take Doerr's hand. Nor did the latter, spitting on his palm beforehand to seal a bargain, as was the German fashion. Instead the ex-U-boat officer said, "You can start on the next shift tomorrow morning, digging. You'll need some sort of hat and a pair of long-johns, they're the easiest to get off quickly, in case the Tommy ferrets start nosing about."

"Yes, I know. I've been there before."

Over in the darkening compound, the staff sergeant in charge was shrilling on his whistle. "Lock-up . . . five minutes to lock up," Doerr said, as if the Hard Man didn't know.

The other man grunted something and then, without another word, he started to wander back to his own hut,

Doerr forgotten already. For his devious mind was full of his own burgeoning plan.

As he thought of it now, walking slowly through the growing darkness, listening to the rattle of the dixies and tins in the Tommy cookhouse and half conscious of the terrible odour of cabbage they were always cooking, he considered. He hadn't the slightest bit of interest in helping Doerr and the other Blacks to escape. Indeed, if his plan worked out, they would not escape at all. He smiled to himself at the thought.

One of the guards on the tower was shouting to a mate below, "Can't I borrow yer talc, Charlie? I like to whip some between me legs when I'm off out looking for tarts. There's a real hot number at the Rose and Crown. She's worth saying a prayer or two for afterwards."

"Ay," his mate answered grimly, "and she'll be worth getting yer arse shot full of that new pencillin once they discover the pox she's given yer!"

Hard Man wasn't listening. He was concentrating on the task at hand. So that he could carry out his own private plan, he'd need to know just how far Doerr and the rest of the idiots had got with their tunnel. More importantly, he *had* to know when they were going to break out to the surface. That was crucial.

He sniffed, catching a whiff of that terrible cabbage which the Tommies served with those equally awful Brussels sprouts all the time. That knowledge would help him to succeed in his own attempts. He knew he was a marked man. Harkins and his spies in the camp would be watching him all the time from now onwards. He had to have a distraction. When the time came he wanted the Tommies to concentrate solely on the Doerr group. It was the only way he was going to be able to do a bunk. Let the fools play their silly little games with that idiotic tunnel. They deserved to fail, ameteurs that they were. But he *had* to succeed!

He paused suddenly and pressed his square nails into the hard palms of his big paws till it hurt. This would be his last chance. If he failed this time Harkins would ensure that he was sent to that escape-proof 'bad boys' camp' in the wilds of Scotland or have him shipped off to East Africa, the white man's grave, and he would never reach the Homeland to celebrate that final victory and participate in National Socialist Germany's tremendous future.

He stared around at the camp which had been his home for nearly a year and felt a longing for Germany that he had never experienced before.

It was so powerful that it almost hurt physically. He had to get away from this sordid place where there was no hope and no future. Better death than Camp 52 much longer! Head sunk, brutally powerful shoulders jutting forward as if he were about to charge some formidable obstacle, Hard Man ploughed forward through the night, one thought uppermost in his mind: the old motto, 'MARCH OR CROAK!'

A mile or so away, Harkins and his wife shivered in the icy snug, nursing the weak gin; it was the last the landlord would serve them this night. "Gin don't grow on trees, yer know. Them Canucks and Yanks drink places like this dry, yer know."

Harkins, the man who had nearly won the VC, victor of half-a-dozen desperate battles in the trenches, had nodded tamely and said in his best country solicitor's voice, used for calming down irate clients before the war, "I understand fully, landlord. Times are exceedingly hard."

The grumpy old man with his beer belly and petulant

manner had grunted something and shuffled out in his holed carpetslippers, leaving them to enjoy the last of *ITMA*, saying "Not so loud either. Aida" (his peroxided wife who wasn't too old to entertain the sex-starved young Canadians) "has had one of her funny turns. Locked hersen in the bedroom agen."

Harkins had waited till he had gone and then, cocking an ear to the ceiling and the hectic squeaking of rusty bedsprings coming from that direction, said, "Yes, we can hear it. Must have a Canuck MO helping her to get over it. I can just imagine the kind of medicine he's giving her and I bet it isn't Number Nine!"

"Oh, Charles," his wife had chided him, "Don't be so naughty! Perhaps she's tossing in her sleep or something."

He looked across at his wife, with her iron-grey hair crimped into tight curls from the steel rollers she had to use now, because she couldn't afford to go to a hairdresser on a captain's pay, and asked himself whether she could be that naive. She had once threshed the bed like a crazy woman, moaning and groaning with passion when they had first been married, sobbing "More . . . oh for God's sake – *more*. I'll kill you if you stop now!" Now she knitted a lot, talked a great deal about their only son when he had been a little boy, forgetting perhaps that he had been killed in action in North Africa the year before, and was very 'understanding' – sometimes too damned understanding, he cursed to himself. Not that it mattered now. Somehow or other – he didn't know why, for he had never sensed it in the thick of the desperate fighting of the trenches in the old show – he felt he wouldn't survive the war.

He dismissed the matter and listened once more to

the pear-shaped radio and the crackling reception (the landlord had refused adamantly to have it repaired – "Costs money, y'know, Captain"), waiting for the nine o'clock news on the Home Service. Thereafter they would go to their freezing little bedroom.

"Take a memo." Tommy Handley was saying in that brisk northern manner of his. "To all concerned in the Office of Twerps. Take notice that from today, September the twenty-tooth, I, the Minister of Aggravation, have power to confiscate, complicate and commandeer—"

"How do you spell 'commandeer', Mr Handley?"

Tommy considered for a moment before announcing, "Commandeer, let me see." He started to sing, "Comm-on-and-deer, Tommy Handley's wag-time band, comm-on-and-eer . . . !"

Vera simpered and Handley whispered in what was supposed to be a lecherous manner, "I have the power to seize anything on sight!"

"Oh, Mr Handpump – and me sitting so close to you!"

Harkins's wife gave a genteel titter, covering her teeth as if she were afraid to do so.

He sighed. "Strange old war," he remarked to no one in particular.

Chapter Six

"This is the BBC Home Service," the voice came through clear, very much refined pronunication, and upper class. "The News. And this is Alvar Lidell reading it."

Harkins sat up and his wife took out her knitting. Since the loss of her son, killed in action with the Gordon Highlanders, she was no longer interested in the war.

He was. Now as the upper-class announcer commenced, he wondered idly for a moment if the BBC blokes still read the nine o'clock news in dinner jackets, as they had done before the war.

Suddenly his interest in such matters disappeared, for Lidell began with a piece of startling and totally unexpected news. "The Ministry of Information has just announced," the BBC man enunciated in those splendidly clear tones of his, "that a force of German ships passed through the Straits of Dover slightly after midday today."

Harkins gasped and his wife paused in the middle of her cable-stitch to look at him, wondering what had surprised him.

"Oh my God!" the old Captain exclaimed. "That will definitely set the cat among the pigeons!"

"What, dear?"

For a moment or two he was tempted to shout at her,

but he told himself she had given up the war since her son had been killed. It no longer interested her, save as far as it involved him. Her sole concern now was to get back to their house in the country and the steady, unevetful routine of a country solicitor's wife.

"The fact that German ships have passed through the English Channel," he explained to her patiently, as if she were some kind of gentle idiot, "Probably in sight of Dover itself. It's the first time that a foreign navy has cocked a snoot at the Royal Navy since" – desperately he tried to remember the details of his Matriculation history, studied in what seemed now another age – "since the time of the Dutch wars three hundred years or so ago."

"Oh yes," she said mildly, obviously not one bit interested. She put down her knitting. "For our boys overseas, you know," as she always explained when she was asked why she did so. "They need pullovers in North Africa. I think I'll go upstairs, heat some water for the hot-water bottle and snuggle in." She smiled winningly, "Get The bed warm for you. You know just how cold it is up there. I wish the landlord would let us light the gasfire for a few minutes before we turned in. It would make all the difference." She paused, saw he wasn't looking. Then she, too, heard the noise, muted but distinct, coming from outside, wafted in the direction of the rundown pub by the wind that always seemed to blow round the place.

"What's that?" she asked.

"Nothing important," he reassured her, though he knew immediately what the muffled sound was, coming from the direction of the camp. "You pop to bed and I'll have a last pipe outside in the fresh air. You know how the landlord complains if I smoke the pipe inside. Now run along."

"Wrap up well, it's cold," she admonished.

"I will." He limped to get his greatcoat hung from the rusty nail behind the door and put it on to show her he was listening to her advice. But his mind was racing, his wrinkled face set and worried.

Downstairs the bar was heavy with the sweet smell of American cigarettes The landlady had obviously recovered quickly. Big, brassy and loud, she was nearly falling off her stool as the Canadian, half her age, plied her with double gins, her legs spread so that the young soldier could get his greedy hand up between them more easily.

"Your missus has made a speedy recovery, landlord," he said. He couldn't resist turning the knife in the wound, worried as he was.

The landlord muttered something grumpily and shuffled off through the sawdust to the taproom at the rear where the local farmworkers were playing dominoes and selling each other rabbits at black market prices.

He went out into the cobbled yard and shivered a little. His wife had been right: it was a little chilly. He pulled the greatcoat around him more tightly and cocking his head to one side, listened to the faint cheering coming from the POW camp a mile or so away. They'd obviously heard the news. Naturally, the authorities would have attempted to keep it away from them, but, as he had long suspected, they had an illegal radio secreted about the place somewhere. They knew all about Germany's triumph in the Channel. They'd probably heard more detail too from Lord Haw-Haw* or even Radio Berlin.

---

* Renegade Englishman William Joyce broadcasted from Germany until 30 April 1945. Known as 'Lord Haw-Haw' from his affected British upper-class accent. Hanged on 3 January 1946.

The Germans were always quick to seize the propaganda initiative.

He lit his pipe, watching the searchlights poking their fingers of icy white light between the clouds above the camp, and forgot the mass of the German 'Kriegies', as they had called prisoners of war in the last show. Instead he concentrated on Hard Man.

Naturally the man would be highly delighted at the news. Anything to take a rise out of his captors. More than that, Harkins told himself thoughtfully, puffing steadily at the old pipe which had seen him through many a hard day in the 1914–18 trenches, the enemy triumph would encourage him to carry out his own plans; and by now Harkins was sure they included an escape. Why else the exchange of uniforms and the risk of 14 days in the cooler on bread and water for most of the time?

For a moment or two he forgot Hard Man as that old stabbing pain cut into his right groin. Hurriedly he lowered his pipe and leaned against the wall, suddenly feeling nauseated and sick.

Naturally he had been to see 'Number Nine' when the pain had first started. Though he thought he had seen enough medics when they had cut off his leg in the last show, he trusted Number Nine, nick-named after his standard treatment handed out to would-be patients in the sick bay, *Number Nine and Light Duties*.* Number Nine had been a battalion MO in the trenches; he was another old sweat.

"Have you ever vomited blood of late?" the MO had queried after prodding his right side and announcing that his liver was swollen. He had looked sharply at Harkins.

* Laxative and reduced workload.

47

"No," the latter had lied glibly. "Why?" Number Nine had frowned. "I don't know. But stop drinking if you can. I know it's difficult, but if you don't—" He had left the rest of the sentence unfinished and Harkins had guessed that he had something serious for Number Nine to look so grave. After all, the old MO had always maintained somewhat cynically "Ninety per cent of human ailments will go away of their own accord without treatment. The other ten per cent will kill you."

Now, leaning against the damp wall, feeling slightly sick and listening to the muted cheering, Harkins told himself without fear that he probably was suffering from one of that ten per cent. He shook his head and the nauseating pain vanished. He puffed on his pipe and concentrated on the problem at hand for a little while longer.

Then he shivered. It was getting too cold for him. Slowly and thoughtfully he started to thread his way back to the miserable little pub, telling himself that there would probably be all hell to pay in Whitehall this night; heads would roll.

Inside, the saloon bar was empty save for the young, flushed Canadian and brassy blonde; she had her head thrown back in careless abandon, her face flushed an ugly red as she gasped frantically, her frock thrust back to reveal her suspenders and plump, dimpled, naked thighs. The Canadian was working at her frantically, gasping too like a fiddler's bitch, as Harkin's remembered the old saying.

He raised his pipe cynically in salute. "Turned out nice again," he said, echoing George Formby's famous phrase.

They didn't even notice.

Five minutes later he was cuddled up next to his wife's

cold bottom, eyes closed tightly as if to blot out the rest of that day. But he couldn't sleep. Finally the landlord sounded his bell and proclaimed his time-honoured phrase to an empty pub, for Aida, his wife, and the Canadian had already disappeared to some dark corner of the place. "Time, gentlemen, *please.*" Harkins drifted off into a troubled sleep. He tossed and turned, his wrinkled old body lathered in sweat, gasping as he had just run a race. The blood was pounding from his ruined mouth in the nightmare and an anxious Number Nine was saying over and over again, *"Light duties . . . light duties!"* Behind the two old men, Hard Man stood, smoking pistol in his big paw snarling, *"Huns . . . why do they call us Huns?"* Then it was dawn, with the bugles already sounding Reveille over at the camp when he finally drifted into a peaceful sleep. Under his grizzled head there was blood on the rumpled pillow . . .

Chapter Seven

Grimly, the old man with the face of an occidental Buddha who had lived too well, read through the final sentence in 'The Thunderer'* once again, half-moon spectacles perched at the end of his stubby nose; and what he read there he didn't like one bit.

German Vice-Admiral Otto Ciliax has succeeded where the Duke of Medina Sidonia failed . . . nothing more mortifying to the pride of sea power has happened in Home Waters since the seventeenth century.

"Pah!" the old man cried in exasperation. With an angry gesture he crumpled up the thin, wartime *Times* and flung it to the paper-littered floor of his office. "Absolute rubbish . . . balderdash!" he cried to no one in particular. "Ought not to have been published."

But in his heart he knew that the anonymous *Times* leader writer was justified in his stinging critical comment. The Huns had sailed a fleet of ships, at least two dozen of them of all displacements, right through the Channel – the *English* Channel – and all the might of the Royal

---

* *The Times* newspaper.

Naby and the Royal Air Force had been unable to stop them. No wonder the man in the street would soon be howling for blood. Soon he was going to have to face a couple of unpleasant hours at the Dispatch Box in the House of Commons.

Naturally the man in the street was right. The Huns had been a jump ahead of the Admiralty right from the start of the whole operation. They had done the completely unexpected for a nation which was supposed to be wooden and rigid in its way of thinking. Taking a huge risk, they had jammed and fooled British radar and had shown the world that Britain's pride, its Senior Service, as it liked to call itself, had little ability to improvise when faced with a surprise situation.

Angry still, he pressed the buzzer on his littered desk.

"Sir," the voice of John Colville, his private secretary, came across the intercom immediately.

"Is he there?" he asked. Abruptly the old man realised he had forgotten to put his false teeth in again after lunch. He took them out of his silk monogammed handkerchief, dipped them swiftly in the glass of brandy on the desk in front of him and stuffed them into his toothless mouth. He was ready. In that voice which had thrilled the nation over the past two years when Britain had suffered defeat after defeat, he asked, "Is he there already?"

"Yes, PM. He's waiting in the ante-room."

"Then send him in immediately, John," Winston Churchill boomed. "There is work, urgent work, to be done."

Commodore First Class, Lord Louis Mountbatten, Chief of the newly formed Combined Operations Command, came bounding into the PM's office with the same energy and determination that had made him a feared opponent on

51

the polo field in pre-war days and an outstanding wartime destroyer skipper. He gave the old man behind the desk an immaculate salute and waited expectantly.

Churchill took his time. He sized up the handsome naval officer standing in front of him, telling himself he liked the cut of Mountbatten's jib. Of course, he knew Mountbatten's pre-war image had been that of a wealthy Mayfair playboy who had married into Jewish money. All the same the 'playboy' had proved himself in the fighting in the Meditenanean. Off Crete he had fought his destroyer *Kelly* to the end until she had gone down, all guns still blazing. Here was the man he wanted: an aristocratic officer, used to command, who combined energy, brains and determination.

"Sit down, Mountbatten, pray," he ordered.

Mountbatten sat. He reached instinctively for the silver cigarette case in his pocket. Then he thought better of it. Of old he knew Churchill could be offended by the slightest movement if it broke his concentration. And it was obvious at this moment that the PM was concentrating.

Outside in the Mall the grey barrage balloons bobbed up and down in the breeze like tethered elephants.

"No doubt you have read *The Times* first leader of this morning, Mountbatten," Churchill broke the heavy silence at last.

"Yessir. A real stinker."

"A real stinker indeed," the PM agreed somewhat glumly. "Not to put too fine a point on it, we've been kicked in the arse rather hard. Right in our own backyard. You can imagine what Herr Hitler is making of it. The airways must be full of the boasting of Dr Goebbels this morning. Dammit, he has cocked a snoot at the Royal Navy and got away with it!"

"Yes, I know, sir," Mountbatten said, a note of sympathy in his voice. He knew how much Churchill felt for the Royal Navy and its traditions. After all, the Senior Service had been Churchill's first ministerial office after a decade in the political wilderness before the war. "It won't happen again, sir," he tried to reassure the crestfallen old man. "I'm sure a few heads are rolling this day in Signals and Communications."

"Many, I hope," Churchill said darkly. "I've taken care of that. But what happened in the Channel is already ancient history. We have to think of the conduct of future operations. What do you know of the *Tirpitz?*" he asked in a surprising change of direction.

"The *Tirpitz*, sir? Why, sir, she's Germany's largest remaining battleship since we sank the *Bismarck*, her sister ship, last year."

"Exactly. She's probably the biggest battleship in the world. She has a displacement of 45,000 tons and her speed makes her faster than all of our capital ships, including our latest, the *Prince of Wales.*"

Mountbatten nodded his agreement, wondering where all this was leading.

"Now, Commodore, you know what a devil of a damned chase that *Bismarck* led us last May. Half the Atlantic and Home Fleets were on her tail, and it cost us the *Hood* with over a thousand casualties. Now you don't need a crystal ball to know what must be going through Herr Hitler's crazed head at this moment after the success of the Channel dash, eh?"

"You don't mean, sir—"

"I do!" Churchill interrupted him. "Intelligence thinks that the *Tirpitz*, locked uselessly away up there in Norway, might well be preparing for a foray into the Atlantic to attack our convoys. Even if Hitler loses her on a venture of that kind, his U-boats will take advantage of her attacks. Why? I'll tell you. Because we'll have to take the Home Fleet off protecting the food convoys vital to the future of this island, to go hunting for the *Tirpitz*." He frowned hard, as if for the first time he was realising exactly what that meant. "The result?" He shrugged. "The U-boats will have a field day with our undefended convoys and I don't need to tell you, Mountbatten, just how serious that would be. The country's on the verge of starving as it damn well is."

Churchill sighed like a man bearing the cares of the world on his shoulders and stared glumly out at the grey, ugly slugs of the barrage balloons. Abruptly Mountbatten, an unemotional man, felt a sense of compassion for this toothless old man nearing 70, upon whom the fate of the British Empire rested. "But sir," he said, trying to cheer the PM up, "Once the *Tirpitz* is out in the Atlantic – she'll never get back again. Their Lordships, God bless them – have learned from the *Bismarck* affair last year. Once the *Tirpitz* goes on the rampage they'll seal off the Denmark Strait between Greenland and Iceland with subs and aircraft from our carriers. She'll never get back to Norwegian waters, I'm sure of that, sir."

Churchill leaned forward and pointed his big double Corona at the handsome young naval officer like an offensive weapon, almost accusingly. "And that's exactly what Herr Hitler wants."

"What do you mean, sir?"

"I mean that the *Tirpitz* will not attempt to get back to Norwegian waters as their Lordships might well expect her to do."

"How do you mean, sir? Where will she go?" Mountbatten

asked, puzzled. "There are only a few ports in the West that can accommodate a ship of her size."

By way of an answer, Churchill rose to his feet and stomped with the aid of his cane to the big wall map of Europe which adorned one side of the room. Suddenly Mountbatten's eyes lit up. He and his commandos had already guessed what the PM had in mind but for the moment he said nothing. Instead, he waited for Churchill to make the announcement which he now expected. The PM looked at the big map dotted with red and blue flags indicating the Allied and enemy dispositions. Suddenly, he stabbed his nicotine-stained forefinger at it, jowls wobbling with the effort. "That's where she'll head for once the chase has commenced . . . *St Nazaire!*"

Mountbatten could hardly restrain his excitement. He had always aimed at being a winner throughout his naval career. It looked as if he had won yet again.

Unaware of what was going through Mountbatten's mind, Churchill said, "I can see that you're following my train of thought, young man."

"I certainly am, sir," Mountbatten said triumphantly, No longer able to contain himself. "My chaps, the commandos, are already working on it."

"On what, pray?"

"Preparing for a raid on that very same port."

"You mean St Nazaire?"

"I do indeed, sir."

"Well, I live and breathe, Mountbatten!" Churchill gasped, surprised for once, for a man who was never surprised. But he pulled himself together with "Tell me more in a moment, Mountbatten. But let's make it clear from the outset: I don't want *Tirpitz* running

55

wild in the Atlantic and then safely making her way to St Nazaire where she would be a constant threat. Our cousins across the sea" – he meant the Americans – "would not be impressed by that one bit. Indeed it might swing them against us so much that President Roosevelt would be unable to bring them into the war on our side. The Americans have no patience with a loser. In short, my dear young man, we must discourage the Huns from even thinking of bringing the *Tirpitz* out of her Norwegian berth to make a run for it into the Atlantic."

"And that's why I'm here, sir?"

"Yes," Churchill answered without hesitation, knowing that a commander who could plan ahead like Mountbatten, as vain as he was and constantly searching to be in the limelight, was the only man to lead an operation of this kind. "If that madman Herr Hitler has no port for the *Tirpitz* to run to in the end I think he would be foolish to send her out on a suicide mission without any hope. No, Herr Hitler," he shook his head significantly, "is not *that* mad."

"My role, sir?"

"Your role is to ensure that your commando chappies destroy the port of St Nazaire well in advance. All the harbour facilities must disappear overnight so that there is nowhere along the whole of the Atlantic coast that could accommodate the *Tirpitz* when she could be taken care of with supplies, repairs, rearmament and the like."

"I see, sir," Mountbatten said somewhat woodenly now, as if for the first time he had fully realised the extent of an operation against St Nazaire, as strongly fortified as the port was, with half-trained 'hostilities only'* marine commandos and the new rookies in the commandos. "And, sir, when do you expect Combined Operations Command to carry out this mission?"

Churchill looked up at him gravely, knowing as always on such occasions that the words he would now use might well condemn scores of young men to an early and violent death and others to years of prolonged suffering as cripples and permanent invalids. But he said it all the same; he had to. "When? Without delay. *St Nazaire must cease to exist as a deepwater naval port by the end of next month, Mountbatten!*"

---

* Men who have joined the Navy, and the other services for the war period – hostilities – only.

BOOK TWO

ESCAPE TO DEATH

Chapter One

Hard Man pored over the little, faded pre-war map once again. As he squatted all by himself in the latrine – the 'thunderboxes', due to the noise and noxious smell coming from them – the one place in the camp where the bored POWs, with all the time in the world on their hands, did not linger. Here one could be alone – if one could stand the odour – and at this present moment, Hard Man was too excited even to notice it. The stolen map was too much of a treasure.

Yet once again he had run the risk of another spell in the cooler on bread and water to exchange places with an ordinary seaman in order to get outside on a working party. He had picked a broad-faced ex-Hamburger docker for the exchange. '*Hein Muck*', as he liked to call himself after a well-known character in Hamburg's red-light district, had accepted his offer without the slightest hesitation. In a voice thickened by years of cheap *Korn* – schnapps – and even cheaper cigars, he had replied, "I'm yer man, *Herr Leutnant*. I wouldn't mind playing a lah-de-da officer and gent for a day, without the problems. All them mess stewards in their white jackets waiting on yer hand and foot and finger bowls after yer've had yer fodder of an evening. Lead me to it, *Herr Leutnant*, toot-sweet." He had given Hard Man the benefit of his schnapps-ridden smile.

Hard Man hadn't enlightened him. Indeed he had to hold back his annoyance when the ex-docker had quipped on parting, "Is it true, sir, that officers and gents actually fart through their ribs, not like us common folk?"

The map find had come about totally unexpectedly. It had been almost as if some god on high had decided to help him in his escape and place the precious document in his path.

It had started with the usual tip-and-run raider. They visited the coast around Southampton all the time now as their victory in the Channel had emboldened the *Luftwaffe* High Command into believing that England was just about finished. The lone fighter-bomber had come in at tree-top height, ripping slugs the length of the battered pre-war passenger train carrying the POWs and their guards for another day's work at the docks. Almost immediately the frightened driver and his mate had braked and thrown themselves into the leafless winter bushes at the side of the track, to the accompaniment of the POWs' scornful cheers.

Thereafter time had passed leadenly. The lone tip-and-run raider had disappeared in the direction of Southampton, over which dark plumes of smoke were already beginning to rise. But the sirens had yet to sound the All Clear and Hard Man knew from past experience that trains were forbidden to move while an air raid was underway.

In the corridorless, shabby train, which obviously hadn't seen a lick of paint since before the war, the cooped-up POWs started to get restless. As usual the camp latrines had been blocked before they had set off – there was nothing new in that. They often were just after breakfast when the men poured the hated porridge down them. Now Nature had commenced worrying them as their bowels rumbled and their bladders began to fill up. They started to stamp their feet impatiently, rattle at the locked windows, tagging at the leather straps to see if they could lower the glass, crying angrily or pitifully, "Hey, let me off, I want a shit! Have a friggin' heart, Tommy, let me get to the shithouse. The piss is trickling down my leg into my boot. Christ, now I've gone and wet my breechess, you buck-toothed Tommy barnshitter!"

Finally the middle-aged guards had relented. Herding the POWs forward at the tip of their bayonets, they had moved them into the abandoned station, stinking of dust and cat's urine. Rats had scampered out of their path as the men had scattered and rushed the lavatories, bearing the fading legends 'Ladies' and 'Gents', with the admonition on the door of the latter urging the user, 'Please adjust your dress before leaving'.

Hard Man had urinated in a firebucket filled with rock-hard sand; unable as always to tolerate the mob all around him he was strangely shy of revealing his genitals to others, even if they were his fellow men. Idly he had wandered around the long-abandoned place with its fading notices informing the reader 'What To Do If War Comes'. That had made him smirk; the war had come a long while before and the Tommies were patently losing it.

But the smirk soon vanished when he had first set his eyes on the fading poster, depicting a leggy blonde in a skimpy swimsuit, throwing a multi-coloured beachball, with the wording advising, 'Come to breezy Brighton and Enjoy Yourself!' For below the pre-war poster there was a map of the South Coast, with beyond, clearly outlined, *that of France!*

He had looked around quickly. But the POWs were too busy jostling and pushing to get into the lavatories and the bored guards, knowing that their charges were otherwise occupied, were already tucking into their haversack rations, great hunks of greasy corned beef and stale cheese stuffed between slices of grey wartime bread, their precious 'wads'.

Hard Man had hesitated no longer. With a swift glance to left and right, he had pulled the poster down and secreted it inside the blouse of his battledress. The customary search on return to camp had been easy. He had made it obvious he had been carrying contraband as he was stopped at the gate and the guards had found the stolen oranges from the split crate almost immediately. Hard Man knew there would be no trouble from the Tommy. He wouldn't report the theft because those stolen oranges would be scoffed by his children that night or exchanged at the local pub for a pint of wallop, as the Tommies called beer. The triumphant Tommy hadn't even thought of searching him any further, when he might have discovered the map.

Now as he pored over it in the growing darkness of the wooden latrine, with the rats scuttling and pawing their way through the yellow ordure below, he considered, fitting the pieces of the jigsaw together slowly and patiently.

Back in that heady, victorious summer of 1940, he and the rest of his U-boat flotilla had toured the newly conquered French Atlantic ports, watched by the sullen, pouting *Pom-poms rouges* of the defeated French Navy. Their brief had been given to them by hatchet-faced Admiral Doenitz, the commander of the U-boat Army. He had assembled them on the quay at Kiel just before the flotilla had sailed and, his mouth working as if on steel springs, barked: "Comrades, fellow U-boat men. You think the conflict is over. It isn't! That Jew Roosevelt in Washington is intent on bringing America into the war, urged on by those Jewish plutocrats of his. He will continue to supply the Tommies with weapons and food. There will be rich pickings when they sail their convoys across the Atlantic *if we are waiting for the Amis!*" He had emphasized the words. "But to do so we need good bases on the Atlantic coast out of the immediate reach of Churchill's navy. *You* will find those safe bases."

So they had toured the French ports, whoring and drinking for the most part, but always on the lookout for a good berth. They had been to Dieppe, St Malo, Brest, Lorient and the like. All had been quite suitable. But two of the French ports had been declared off-limits for the U-boat Army. They had been Brest and St Nazaire. It had been explained to them that these ports, with their deep-water anchorages, had been reserved for the German Navy's larger surface ships.

Now, as he squatted in the latrine, he thought again of that dying commando, trying to get out the French name, as he slumped there in a pool of his own blood on the dockside. "*Saint . . .*" he had gasped, his body racked by death agonies, so that he had been unable to think straight. Hard Man stared at the map, though he didn't need to. He had already guessed the Tommy had meant St Nazaire. There was no other large port with the 'Saint' prefix on that section of the coast.

He stared at the hessian screen which enclosed the latrine as if he might find the answer to his problem printed there. But what would the commandos be training for in connection with St Nazaire?

Abruptly he remembered the great news of the previous night, personally related by Dr Goebbels, 'the

Poisoned Dwarf' to the German people.* The flight of the *Scharnhorst* and the *Gneisenau* meant that from now onwards the Tommies would be watching the French port day and night. Any German ship trying to enter it wouldn't have a chance. It would be blasted out of the water, even before the port boom was raised to allow it in.

He sat back on the hard wooden seat, map held carelessly in his big paw, as the last piece in the jigsaw fell into place with surprising case. It was obvious. The Tommies were going to take St Nazaire out of commission; that's what the dying commando had been training for. Without the last remaining deep-water port, suitable for a battleship, at their disposal, the German Naval High Command would be unable to send a surface raider into the Atlantic. For once the Tommies had located her and she was forced to make a run for port, as had happened to the ill-fated *Bismarck* in 1941; there would be no place of safety for her. The surface raider would be forced to take on the whole might of the British Home and Atlantic Fleets and be battered to her death mercilessly, the same fate that had befallen the *Bismarck*.

Hard Man bit his bottom lip. His plan to steal a small boat off Southampton was well advanced. That would be no problem. There were plenty of pre-war small craft for the taking left beached there on the coast. Nor would there be any difficulty in getting out of the camp, though this time he couldn't leave dressed as a German other rank. This time it would have to be a full-blown escape, with every man's hand against him.

The problem was making time for himself. He needed,

* German Minister of Propaganda, known as such because of his vitriolic tongue and small size.

he estimated, at least 24 hours on the outside before the hue-and-cry was raised. By then he hoped and prayed he would have found his small craft and be on his way to the nearest landfall in German-occupied Europe, where he would report his exciting and vital information. He hoped that it would mean promotion, a medal and above all his own command. Now, after nearly a year in Tommy captivity, he yearned to take revenge for all the snubs and insults he had suffered in that time. Now he burned to teach the buck-teeth Tommies that never again would they call the Germans Huns.

Outside, the guards were beginning to shrill their whistles urgently. It was five minutes to lock-up. Already Doerr and his tunnelling crew would be getting ready for a night's work underground. Their flagging energy had been renewed now that they were only metres away from the spot outside the wire through which they had planned to break out. All they were waiting for was a dark night.

Hard Man decided it was time to move, in all senses of the word. He had to know how long it would be before Doerr made his decision to break out; that was vital to his plan. He had to get his own escape ready and keep it well hidden, for he was sure that that cunning old fox of an Intelligence Officer, Captain Harkins, would soon attempt to shake him and his possessions down. It would be fatal if his plan were discovered at this late stage. That was something he could not allow to happen. Hurriedly he stowed away his map, as the feet shuffling outside indicated the last of the POWs were abandoning the circuit for another long night of being locked in, passing the hours with dreams of longing that would probably never be realised.

He gave a hard smile in the growing darkness. His dreams *would*, he knew that implicitly. One dawn soon the Tommy commandos would come swarming ashore at St Nazaire, full of piss and vinegar, to be met by a devasting hail of fire. Then at last he would have had his revenge.

Chapter Two

They were all assembled when the two of them, 'Howling Mad' O'Rourke and Second Lieutenant Peter Egan of No. 2 Commando, arrived somewhat flushed and breathless at the door of the great marble conference room, with the solemn marine sentries with fixed bayonets checking passes, guarding the door. As usual the train from the South Coast, its woodwork splintered and patched from the many times it had been shot up on its journeys to London, had been late. "Enemy action," the stationmaster had announced over the echoing, metallic Tannoy system, as if that explained everything. "Bullshit!" 'Howling Mad' had exclaimed, his eyes as red and flaming as his hair, "probably swinging the friggin' lead drinking char in the backroom and planning their friggin' next strike. Christ, what a friggin' war."

Egan, young, handsome and somewhat apprehensive, for after all the CO had a trigger-sharp temper and didn't tolerate fools gladly whatever their rank, had made no comment. He had judged it wiser not to do so.

Now, as they strode into the big, echoing room, Howling Mad's kilt swinging around his brawny calves, his big paw clasping the hilt of his claymore, carried contrary to King's Regulations on officers' dress, the commando major looked fiercely to left and right as if challenging any

69

of the illustrious, high-ranking officers present to make a comment. None dared do so. They kept their gaze fixed studiously on the dais to their front.

They were all there: the future cowards, the dead men and those who would win their country's highest award before that month was out. The Combined Operations briefing room was packed with familiar and unfamiliar faces (at least to the young Canadian Peter Egan). There were officers in the blue of the Senior Service, the khaki of every commando currently stationed in the United Kingdom, the dark uniforms of the Free French, the blue-grey of the Royal Air Force, with here and there the khaki and pink trousers of the observers from the United States, presently in Britain.

As the two of them took their seats next to a bearded Commander Beattie, the skipper of the Lend-Lease,* obsolete destroyer HMS *Campbeltown*, which would play a vital role in what was soon to come, Howling Mad growled in what he regarded as a whisper, though his words could be heard right through the big room: "All the brass hats, young Egan. Hope they can friggin' fight as well as they can friggin' waffle, eh!"

Everyone heard the comment, but none of them made any protest. They all knew Major O'Rourke and his unpredictability.

Egan looked furtively around the room at the important officers, and told himself that the whole gang was here. Everyone he knew in Combined Ops, and some he didn't, were present. Obviously the balloon was going to go up somewhere or other; and he was glad of it. He had

---

* Destroyers loaned to Britain by President Roosevelt from America's mothball fleet in return for concessions in the British West Indies.

been waiting almost three years now in this chilly, wet, undernourished England for his first taste of action: the reason he had volunteered for the Canadian Army in the first place. Now it looked as if he was going to see some at last.

A moment later Mountbatten strode in. Someone cried, "Cigarettes out, chaps!" Almost immediately Mountbatten, standing handsome, proud and erect on the dais, announced: "Gentlemen, let me say from the outset that this is not an ordinary raid of the kind some of you have taken part in previously. *This is a real operation of war!*"

Immediately, an electric ripple of excitement ran through his audience. It was clear now why they had been summoned here so surprisingly from all over the UK. this was going to be a really big one. They leaned forward expectantly.

Mountbatten didn't keep them on tenterhooks. He clicked his fingers. A commando captain, wearing a cap and with a holstered revolver strapped to his webbing belt, responded immediately. He tugged back the black cloth covering the big map on the easel to the left side of the dais.

"*St Nazaire!*" Mountbatten snapped, without preliminaries. "This is going to be the target of your Tenth Anti-Submarine Striking Force, at a date which I will reveal to you later."

"Never heard of it," O'Rourke growled. "Tenth Anti-Submarine Striking Force." What the hell is that when it's at home?" But there was no one present seemingly prepared to answer that puzzled question.

Mountbatten held his hands up to silence the excited chatter that had broken out after his announcement, the look on his handsome face half-amused, half quizzical.

"St Nazaire," he said, "where the River Loire joins the Atlantic Ocean, is a port of some fifty thousand souls, It is two hundred and fifty miles from the British harbour of Falmouth." Swiftly he sketched in how the *Bismarck* had attempted and failed to reach the port the previous May. Now, as he explained, the PM feared her sister ship would try to do the same, once the *Tirpitz* had finished her battle cruise in the North Atlantic.

"So, gentlemen," Mountbatten said, as Peter Egan felt a rising sense of excitement at being in on such great events, though he hadn't the slightest idea of what his own personal role would be, "to make sure the *Tirpitz* will not do the same and attempt to leave her Norwegian refuge, we must take preliminary action."

He paused to let his words sink in. All was silent now save the heavier breathing of the portly senior officers and the steady tread of the sentries' hobnail boots on the marble floor outside in the echoing nineteenth-century corridor.

"How are we going to do so?" Mountbatten answered his own question: "Like this. We shall destroy St Nazaire's port facilities, in particular the great dry dock, *Forme Ecluse* – here," he pointed to the map. "Or to be more accurate, the great gates – here – which give access to the dock. Once they are destroyed, there is no other port on the French Atlantic coast which can accommodate the Hun monster."

"Bloody cheek!" Howling Mad whispered to Peter Egan, "He's a bloody Hun himself!"

The young Canadian ignored the stage whisper, which everyone around them obviously heard. He thought it wiser to do so.

"Now what are the difficulties of an operation of this kind?"

Mountbatten answered his own rhetorical question. "One," he ticked the point off on his well-manicured nail. The port of St Nazaire is six miles up the River Loire. That is six miles deeper into German-occupied territory than Combined Ops have ever been before. That's why I call it *not* a raid, but an operation of war.

"Difficulty number two. The approach to St Nazaire is by a deep-water channel running across the lee of the north bank of the River Loire. Most of that length is defended by heavy German coastal batteries. South of that is a wide area of mudflats covered only at deep water. According to the backroom boys, the high spring tide at the end of March would give us just enough water for our motor-launches – and possibly destroyers too if they weren't too heavily laden."

Egan looked at Howling Mad. The latter frowned, as if realising for the first time how dangerous an op of this kind would be.

"Finally," Mountbatten went on, "difficulty number three. The distance the assault force would have to cover, and bear in mind the range of the average motor-launch which will be going in with us. The nearest harbour would be – here – at Falmouth in Cornwall. That would mean a round trip of five hundred miles. I think – and I'm sure you'll agree, gentlemen – that's a devilishly long trip for the average ML. At the end of it, its fuel tanks would be virtually empty." He paused. "Naturally, there is a very strong possibility that the Boche might discover the assault force on its way to the objective and I'm sure the Huns would harass the convoy on its way back. They would be in an excellent position to do so, especially if your craft had taken hits and were forced to slow down, which is quite likely."

"If, we come back" O'Rourke muttered grimly.

In front of him a senior general turned and glared hard at the speaker. O'Rourke glared back. Peter Egan told himself he didn't know how Howling Mad O'Rourke had survived so long; he was always cocking a snoot at the brass hats.

Mountbatten cleared his throat noisily with an air of finality, as if he couldn't – wouldn't – say much more. "Well, gentlemen," he said, "those are the difficulties. Let us see what we propose to do about them, shall we?" He extended his hand to the burly commando colonel puffing his unlit pipe thoughtfully in the front row of the hard-backed wooden army chairs. "Colonel Newman, would you like to take over now?"

The commando officer stuffed his pipe away hastily into the pocket of his battledress blouse and, with surprising agility for a man of his age and bulk, sprang onto the platform next to Mountbatten. He was obviously tremendously fit.

"Thank you, sir. Well, gentlemen, let me say this from the very start. The chap who planned this op deserves the OBE for sheer damned audacity!"

There was a rumble of muted laughter and O'Rourke said sourly, "Ay, he would. OBE – *Other Buggers' Efforts!*"

Egan smiled as Charles Newman, who was obviously quite a character, continued. "Now the drill so far as the Army goes. Men from my own Second Commando and 80 men from every commando in the UK, each one a demolitions expert, will sail for St Nazaire, with the aid of Ryder's craft." He grinned down at the Lieutenant Commander, the Commander of the 10th Anti-Submarine Striking Force. Newman was obviously pleased to have Ryder and his ships in their place; they were simply to be the means of transporting the real fighting men to the scene of the action.

The knowledge must have pleased O'Rourke for he growled sourly, "Senior Service, my aching arse! I've shat those types before brekker."

Egan made no comment.

"So while the Brylcreem boys" – he meant the RAF pilots – "drop their eggs on the Jerries to create a diversion, my chaps will land from the motor-launches. It will be their task to knock out the Jerry coastal batteries, destroy the sub pens and generally raise bloody hell in the dock area." So saying, and without another word, he dropped into his seat and took out his battered old pipe once more.

Mountbatten rose to his feet again. "Thank you, Colonel Newman," he said. "Now, Commander Ryder. Can I call upon you to explain the Navy's part in this op?"

Ryder, a good-looking officer with an aggressive jaw, rose, stuck his hands deeply into his pockets and stared around in baleful silence for a few moments. It was as if he were surveying a particularly sloppy ship's crew from his quarter deck and not particularly liking what he saw.

He cleared his throat loudly. It meant 'Pay attention, you bunch of land-lubbers, a member of the Senior Service is addressing you!'

"Now the naval attack force has this job. One HMS *Campbeltown*, commanded by Commander Beattie, will ram the dock gate at *Forme Écluse*." Ryder ignored the excited buzz among his audience which greeted his announcement. Without pause, he went on: "Of course, ramming dock gates is not the sort of naval exercise which one can practise very frequently! So we can't be certain if the *Campbeltown* will pull it off completely. To make doubly certain, therefore, she will be carrying five tons of high explosive in her bows. On a delayed charge. That, the boffins think, should do the trick."

He cleared his throat once more.

"Thought the Senior Service supped pink gin all day," Rourke snorted. "What's wrong with the chap, clearing his bloody throat all the time like that?"

"Two. The assault force," Ryder went on, "will sail in three columns. The midships one will consist of my own ship, the *Atherstone, HMS Tynedale* and, of course HMS *Campbeltown*, plus Motor Gun Boat 314. The two port and starboard columns will carry Colonel Newman's brown jobs," he grinned at his slip of the tongue.* "I mean his commandos, 265 men in all. Any questions, gentlemen, so far?"

There were none, so Ryder strode purposefully to the map. "Now the naval force," he continued, "is faced by two major dangers, presupposing that the task force gets into the mouth of the Loire without being spotted. One, the coastal guns running along here from the Old Mole to the entrance of the *Forme Écluse*. As you've already heard, Colonel Newman's chaps will take care of those guns. Two, Intelligence reported yesterday that the Huns have suddenly bethed four *Moewe*-class destroyers – here – in the *Avant Port*. I should imagine that they will present no initial danger as we sail in." He frowned hard. "But they *could* provide us with one hell of a headache on the way out. All right, gentlemen?"

Egan liked Ryder. To the young Canadian he seemed down-to-earth, not given to airs and graces. His exposé finished, he vacated the platform immediately to that

---

* Naval slang for the brown-uniformed British Army.

obvious smoothie, Mountbatten, who dearly loved, it was clear, to perform before an audience.

Mountbatten smiled winningly at his audience. "In essence, gentlemen, the whole operation depends upon our getting into position before the Boche has woken up to the fact that he is being attacked. Once the *Campbeltown* has rammed the dock gate and the commando is ashore, there is little that the Boche can to but to react. For we will have already acted, decisively I hope. So what does it all boil down to, gentlemen? I shall tell you – absolute, total security. The assembly harbour should be fairly safe from enemy aerial reconnaissance." He looked hard at his listeners. "My guess is that the danger to this operation will come not from above, from the *Luftwaffe*, but from *within* – spies, agents, in other words. We've provided a cover story for the Tenth Anti-Submarine Force naturally. It is intended to carry out long-range sweeps far beyond the Western Approaches. As for the commandos, as soon as they arrive at Falmoath they will be issued with sun helmets, khaki drill for the tropics and the like. In other words they are supposed to be on their way to the East."

Mountbatten let his words sink in before saying, "From this moment onwards, no soldier or sailor will be allowed to leave his unit, whatever circumstances. If there is a fatality in a man's family and the man applies for compassionate leave, that application will be conveniently forgotten until he returns from the op. If we suffer any deaths during training, as might well occur – we'll be using live ammunition – the dead man will be kept secretly at Devonport Hospital for the time being. Sick personnel, however ill, will treated in the local sick bay. I know these measures will cause heartache, perhaps even severe hardship. But that's not important." His voice hardened and his face was abruptly taut and even ruthless in appearance. "At this stage of the great conflict, gentlemen, *Operation Chariot* cannot fail, not only for military reasons, but also for propaganda ones. We must show the Yanks that we can achieve a victory at last." He shrugged a little helplessly. "If we can't, we'll never bring them into the war on our side."

The handful of American listeners, the observers, looked at each other, amazed at such frankness from the usually stuffy Limeys. But they said nothing as Mountbatten clicked to attention, indicating that the briefing was over.

Without another word, not even a salute as military regulations demanded, they filed out in silence, each man wrapped in a cocoon of his own apprehensions and fears.

Chapter Three

A night bird squawked angrily as if awakened from its
sleep. But almost immediately the bird, hidden somewhere in the skeletal trees around the POW camp was
silent again. Overhead the searchlight explored the inky
sky with its cold fingers of light. Far away, outside the
wire in the NAAFI, the Tommies were bawling drunkenly,
for after all this *was* Saturday night, *"For we're saying
goodbye to them all . . . the long and the short and the
tall . . . yer'll get no promotion this side of the ocean."*
Behind the tight blackout shutters of the prisoners' huts
there was silence.

He guessed that the great majority of his fellow POWs
would already be in their frowsy, double-decker bunks,
eyes closed tightly against the weak yellow light of the
naked electric bulbs, trying to escape the day into sleep
and blessed oblivion.

But Hard Man crouched in the shadows, tense and alert,
heart beating a little faster than normal, knowing that not
all of his fellow POWs slept. Tonight, those fools and
idiots of tunnelers would make their attempt to escape. It
was Saturday night and they assumed that the Tommies
would be relaxing their guard.

"You know the Tommies," one of the would-be escapers
had snorted scornfully at the last briefing of the tunnelers,

"if they're not swilling weak tea, they're downing that awful pissy beer of theirs. God, I'd give my left testicle for a litre of good foaming Munich beer!"

"Well, you'll have some time to wait for that," Doerr had remarked.

"For fuckin' ever, as far as I'm concerned," Hard Man had commented to himself.

All the same, Hard Man now reasoned, as he crouched there surrounded by the still, inky darkness this lonely Saturday night in the middle of World War Two; the men on duty and, especially those in the towers manning the machine-guns and spotlights, would be alert enough. That swine Harkins, the Intelligence Officer, with his damned squeaky pegleg, would see to that. Without the diversion which he prayed would attract the attention of the on-duty Tommies he didn't stand a chance of getting away successfully.

He flashed a glance at the green-glowing dial of his wristwatch. It wouldn't be long now. He groped in the darkness of his smelly sandy burrow for his pack. It lay next to the shabby papier-mâché briefcase bartered for one week's precious cigarette ration. Everything was in place.

He waited again in tense silence. Once more he checked the timing of the middle-aged sentries with their fixed bayonets as they strode up and down outside the last circle of barbed wire. They were supposed by regulations to keep a silent watch, not speaking with one another. Naturally they didn't; it would have been too boring for hours on end. So at the end of each beat they exchanged a few whispered words with one another, which in that empty silence carried a long way. Now, again, he heard the harsh scratch and rasp, followed by the sudden blue flare of a match being lit as they had a furtive 'spit-and-draw' as they called it in their own slang. So, he could pinpoint them quite clearly.

Over at the NAAFI they were bellowing. *"Now I've got her on the run . . . roll me over in the clover . . . roll me over lay me down and do it again!"*

Hard Man pulled a face. What a coarse, vulgar people the English were; always concerned with 'Number One', as they called sex. He dismissed the dirty ditty and concentrated once again on the task at hand.

Again Hard Man flashed a look at his wristwatch. Time was pushing on, though slowly. Naturally he knew the escapers' plan by now; he had been working for them, keeping his ears open and saying little, for over a week now. They intended to start breaking through to the surface outside the wire 20 minutes before the sentries changed. Five minutes or so before the change, they would make a break for it. Doerr had reasoned to them that by then the Tommy sentries would have one thing on their minds – getting out of the night cold, downing a cup of hot cocoa in the warm fug of the guardroom and getting their heads down in their bunks for four hours until their next spell of guard duty. "By the time the next guard is alerted to march out," he had concluded, "I want all of us who are escaping under the exit and ready to move. One man out every 30 seconds. We'll be gone and into the woods before the new sentries'll have found their bearings, comrades," he had ended confidently. "Then it's off and home to mother."

Hard Man's face looked wolfish and very dangerous in the thin light coming from the lantern over the gate. That's what Doerr thought, he told himself. There'd be no 'home to mother' for him this side of Christmas – and it would serve the fool right. He deserved a nasty shock. All those men playing their foolish games did; they had it coming to them.

He sat back on his heels in the frozen turf, covered by the skeletal trees of the wood. Time passed leadenly. "Come on!" he urged fiercely to no one in particular. Now that the time was near for his own escape, after he had taken so long in its planning, he wanted to be on his way and leave Camp 57 behind him for good. Again he flashed a look at his wristwatch. His heart skipped a beat. *It was time!*

He levered himself to his feet, nerve ends tingling, feeling the adrenalin surging through his veins. He was ready for action – for anything. Now, he knew, they'd he pushing their way through the last metre of the shaft, the trolleys which carried them down the narrow earthern tunnel rolling back and forth noiselessly on their greased wooden wheels.

"*Jetzt–los!*" He heard the urgent whispered command quite clearly on the still night air, and tensed. They were coming out! There was no time to waste. It was now or never. He pulled out the long metal whistle which he had stolen from the Tommy guardhouse, put it to his lips and waited for the head of the first escaper to appear from below. Suddenly there it was. Under other circumstances it would have looked foolish: a head like that of a human mole, peering anxiously from left to right in the gloom. Not now. This was life or death and as far as Hard Man was concerned it didn't matter if it turned out to be the latter.

He hesitated no longer. He raised the whistle to his suddenly dry lips. The suspense and tension of the moment were beginning to have their effect. He spat and then thrust the whistle into his mouth. Puffing his lungs full of cold night air, he blew, once . . . twice . . . three times . . . It was the Tommy alarm signal to be used by all the guards if they needed help in their isolated posts. The shrill sound echoed and re-echoed around the camp.

For a moment nothing happened. Then all hell was let loose. There was an angry shout, followed by another. "What the fuck's going on—" someone began, but the rest of his query was drowned by the sound of heavy hobnailed boots grating down the gravelled path.

Muffled a little by the freshly exposed soil, a German voice called in dismay, *"Grosse Kacke am Christbaum. Die Tommys haben uns gesehen!"*

Hard Man gave an unholy grin. "Great crap on the Christmas tree indeed." The Tommies really had spotted the would-be escapers.

"Stand fast there!" a harsh voice commanded in English.

There was no response. The first POW pulled himself out of the hole and began to run. But not for far. Scarlet, angry flame stabbed the darkness as someone opened up with a sub-machine gun. The running man screamed, high and hysterical. He faltered to a stop. Desperately he flung up his hands. It was as if he were appealing to some god on high for mercy. But his god was looking the other way, for the man dropped and, cursing weakly, died almost immediately on the cropped, frozen turf.

The second POW took in what was happening in an instant. He doubled to the left. Hard Man could hear his hurrying feet, muffled as his shoes were with old socks, running down the gravel track. He didn't get far. A Tommy loomed up out of the darkness, rifle raised. "Cheeky bugger!" he exclaimed angrily. "Stop there!"

Perhaps the POW didn't understand. At all events he didn't stop running. The guard reacted immediately. He slammed his rifle forward. The cruel metal-shod butt smacked into the German's face. He howled with pain and went staggering back, clutching his shattered face, the blood squirting through his fingers.

Hard Man had heard and seen enough. Already there were angry shouts coming from the direction of the inside of the camp itself. Some NCO was bellowing angrily, "Get out of them wanking pits, can't yer friggin' well hear the alarm." In a minute, Hard Man knew they would be sounding the siren and telephoning the Home Guard, Army, and police to warn them of the escape. The pre-arranged cordon would surround the camp in an attempt to stop anyone getting through it.

Crouching low, he doubled for the cover of the wood. Nobody, it seemed, spotted the running figure. The guards were too pre-occupied with the escapers struggling out of the tunnel. Even as he ran, Hard Man could hear Harkins's cool, calm voice calling above the shouts of anger and pain, the crackle of machine-gun fire, the howl of the siren, "Count 'em! . . . Count 'em, immediately, will you!" Hard Man nodded his admiration, although he hated the middle-aged Intelligence Officer passionately. The man was keeping his head in the midst of the mass confusion all around. Harkins wanted to know at once who – if anyone – had got away, so that he could issue an immediate description of the escapee. Naturally he would at once start questioning those POWs who had been recaptured. They would inform the middle-aged Tommy that he had worked in the tunnel but that he was going to none of the places they had agreed to head for and lie up until they continued their escape because Hard

Man had not asked to go out. Apparently he had been just content to help with the digging.

But Hard Man didn't trust Harkins, though he did give him some grudging admiration for being a cunning old fox. Sooner or later the Englishman would be onto his scent and by then he *had* to be undercover, preparing for the last stage of his escape across the Channel with his vital news. Arms working like pistons, breath coming in great hectic gasps, he ran on full-out.

The guard commander was red, flushed, embarrassed and decidedly angry that the Germans had tried to escape while he had been on duty. "Jerry arseholes!" he muttered. "They need a bloody good shafting with something that really hurts."

Harkins smiled sympathetically at the man's honest discomforture. "It could have happened to anybody, Colour Sergeant," he appeased.

"But why yours friggin' truly?" He blew his nose hard.

Next to them, Camp Commandant Colonel Smallpiece – 'Little Dick' to the more irreverent of his men – looked bewildered. But then Smallpiece always looked bewildered. He could well have been born that way, coming out of his mother's womb and blinking uncertainly, as he wondered whether it would be better if he want back in again. "I don't understand all the fuss, Harkins," he stuttered. "We've got most of the rotters back, haven't we? Besides, since these beastly Huns have been coming over here as prisoners, not one of them has managed to do a bunk. After all, we *are* an island, aren't we, Harkins!"

The latter looked at the fat Colonel, whose active service had been limited to acting paymaster in Cologne during the post-World War One occupation of the Rhineland. His contempt was obvious, but he contained himself. There was no use getting angry with idiots. It served no purpose. Instead he said, "Hard Man".

"Oh, him!" For the first time since the escape 'Little Dick' looked a little apprehensive. "What about him, Captain?"

"Well, sir, we've had a bed check – standard operating procedure after a breakout – and we can't find him."

"I say!" the fat Colonel gasped. "Do you think—"

"Yes, I do, sir," Harkins cut him short. "He set his fellow POWs up, sir. He has used them as a cover for his own purposes."

"His own purposes?" the other man echoed, obviously bewildered.

"Yessir," the Intelligence man said patiently though he didn't feel like being patient with the ex-bookkeeper, who didn't look as if he could balance two and two without making five. "The escape party was a diversion while he prepared his own separate escape. All the time Hard Man has been stealing and perhaps bartering – we'll find that out later – with his fellow POWs to get the stuff he'd need on the outside." He paused and let his words sink in, for he knew that 'Little Dick', as the squaddies called him, was slow on the uptake.

Outside, a cockney voice was snarling angrily, "Keep them paws up, yer friggin' square-headed baskets! Or yer'll be lacking a set o' choppers before yer can say friggin' Jack Robinson, mate!"

"But where's he going to escape to, this Hard Man of yours, Harkins?" Little Dick looked worried, as if he had suddenly realised how many tiresome forms and reports he would have to fill in due to this escape. The War Office was mad about deuced reports, he knew.

The other man shrugged wordlessly, his brow furrowed in a worried, perplexed frown.

"More importantly," the Colonel went on pompously, as if Harkins was failing him personally by not having the answers to his questions at the ready, "*Why*? Why is he risking his life in this attempt, which he must know will have no chance of success whatsoever. After all, he could spend months in the cooler for this sort of thing . . ." He ended a little helplessly. "I simply don't understand the logic of the whole damned silly business."

Harkins nodded. "Neither do I, Colonel. All I know is that Hard Man is up to something which make the risks worth while . . . I feel it in my aged bones." His voice rose; his eyes were suddenly determined. "But one thing is for sure, Colonel."

"And what's that?"

"We've got to catch him as soon as possible . . . catch him before he does any damage." Not waiting for any further comment from the puzzled fat Colonel, he rose and touched his hand to the peak of his battered khaki cap in a careless manner, obviously not caring one bit what the other officer thought of him. "You'll excuse me, sir. I must get on." Before the Colonel could protest, he was gone . . .

Chapter Four

"Had a bloody smashing night last night, sir," the commando corporal said sourly to a grinning Peter Egan. "Tommy friggin' Handley on the friggin' wireless agen. Read every bloody paper in the house. The pictures was closed, except for that bloody *In Which We Serve* – and to cap it friggin' all, the missus had her friggin' monthlies agen, or so she said. Freedom in peril, old Winnie said the other day. How bloody right!" He sighed as if sorely tried. "Roll on friggin' death so we can have a go at the friggin' angels!"

"Cheer up, Corp," Peter said, as the ugly, blunt-prowed landing barge bucked up and down on the swell. "It might never happen."

The commando muttered something and fell silent, keeping his eyes on the ugly grey-green seascape to his front. The commando assault force was protected by a destroyer screen while they were on their first exercise for the great new op. All the same, the commandos were on the lookout. German E-boats could come skimming in at 40 knots to launch their lethal tin fish and be on their way again across the Chennel before the destroyers even knew they had attacked.

Time passed boringly as they plodded towards their objective: a river estuary with mud flats on both sides, which according to the boffins resembled the Loire and the entrance to St Nazaire. "They always say that," Howling Mad had snorted in exasperation as that had been explained to him at the pre-exercise briefing. "But on the day it'll all be different. It'll be the usual balls-up and mass confusion. You mark my words, young Egan!"

"Yessir," Peter Egan had replied dutifully and had looked solemn as if he were taking the warning seriously. In fact, his heart was beating faster and his nerves were tingling with excitement at the thought that soon he would be going into action after nearly three years of waiting. God, how long it had all seemed since he had volunteered for the Canadian Army as an 18-year-old back in 1939 and had been forced to tell his crippled father what he had done.

His father, Jess Egan, had gone back to the 'old country', as he always called Britain, in a cattle boat in 1916. Immediately he had been involved in the thick of the fighting on the Western Front from which he had returned a sickly cripple, confined to a wheelchair, living off a meagre government pension so that his long-suffering wife had been forced to open a rooming house in order to make ends meet.

All the same his father had been delighted with the news that his son had volunteered to go overseas. "Get yourself into my old mob, Hell's Last Issue" – he meant the Canadian Highland Light Infantry – "and you'll get your bellyful of fighting, son."

His father, who had died one year later as a direct result of the wounds he had received in the 'Old War', had been badly mistaken. He had gone overseas with the Royal Regiment of Canada straight to a hard-pressed United Kingdom. Already in the crowded trooper taking the volunteers to the 'Old Country', he had the naive young man's visions of heroically winning the country's highest award, the Victoria Cross.

It hadn't worked out that way.

England had not lived up to his expectations. He hadn't minded the grey skies, the persistent rain, the stench of Brussels sprouts and a blacked-out country inhabited by grey, stunted, half-nourished people. His problem had been the lack of action. Instead there had been training, training, training – and yet more training. Week after week, month after month, from one year to the next they had charged up beaches, raced to stick the dummies with their bayonets, yelling wildly, 'bulled up' for CO's parades on a Saturday before going away for the weekend like a bunch of civvies.

The only action the young Canadian had ever seen had been the weekend brawls with the locals in their sawdust-floored pubs or the occasional run-in with the officious Redcaps, hated by both Canadian and British soldier. In the end, and in despair, he had handed in his sergeant's stripes and the pay that went with them and had volunteered for the commandos. After all, *they* were seeing some action, located solely on the fringes of now German-Occupied Europe – Norway, France and the like – but it *was* action nevertheless.

Major 'Howling Mad' O'Rourke, the CO of the commando to which he had been assigned as a private soldier, had taken a shine to the clean-cut, handsome, eager Canadian. Rapidly, thanks to the CO with his unpredictable temper, who in action usually carried bow and arrows for what he called 'silent slaughter', he had been promoted

90

through the ranks until finally, just before he had been let into the secret of the great new op, he had been commissioned: the newest 'one pipper' with a certificate signed by the King-Emperor personally to prove it.

The corporal at the bows, his ruddy, wrinkled face lashed with flying spray, was moaning yet again as he peered through the white gloom. "Couldn't even get the old woman to go to the chip shop last night for one-of-each for me supper," he complained. "Lazy cow! Wouldn't go. I sez to her, 'What's up with you? Yer know I likes me fish and taties on a Friday' – Roman Candles we are, yer see, sir," he added by way of explanation, though privately Peter thought the only time the corporal would go into a church would be to rob the collecting box. "And y'know what she sez, sir? She said she was scared that somebody might molest her in the blackout." He spat over the metal side of the landing barge in contempt. "Molest *her* – that'll be the day!"

Peter Egan laughed at the corporal's righteous indignation. "Total war, Corp, you know. We've all got to make sacrifices wh—"

The words died on his lips and the 'old woman' forgotten immediately; the corporal snapped, "What's up, sir?"

"Look over there – three o'clock," Egan answered, straining his eyes to peer through the grey gloom of flying spray. "Am I seeing things . . . Or is that a Jerry E-boat?"

A hundred yards away in the command barge, bobbing up and down on the swell, Howling Mad O'Rourke had already identified the intruder, nosing its way cautiously into the strung-out commando convoy, "Great balls of fire!" he exploded, his face as furiously red as his hair, "A damned Hun E-boat, right in the middle—" He didn't waste any more breath on explanations. Instead, he pulled the chain on the siren. Immediately it started to shrill its warning across the choppy surface of the Channel.

The E-boat skipper must have heard it, too, and realised that he, the lone raider, had been spotted. With a great roar the E-boat lurched forward. Its razor-edged prow rose out of the sea. Abruptly two white wings of water appeared at its stern. In an instant the area was flooded with the ear-splitting roar of tremendous, high-speed engines going all out.

"Here the bugger comes!" the corporal who had complained about his 'old woman' yelled above that tremendous racket. The 'silly cow' forgotten in a flash, he flung himself behind the Bren gun on the hatch cover to his right. He slammed the butt into his shoulder and, carried away by the wild, unreasoning excitement of battle, yelled exuberantly, "Try this on for friggin' size, you Jerry bastard!" He pressed the trigger of the machine-gun. It spat angry fire and tracer sped lethally towards the heaving, bucking target, gathering speed by the instant.

Egan groaned with frustration. He was armed solely with a .38 revolver. Not much use against a 75-ton E-boat. All the same he felt a sense of sudden admiration for the commandos, who minutes before had been complaining about the need for an exercise on a Saturday, but who were now manning whatever long-range weapons they could find and were blazing away furiously at the enemy craft which was getting larger by the second.

A star shell burst over the stalled convoy. Suddenly their faces were bathed in a glowing, eerie unnatural light.

A moment later the German Oerlikon gunner forrard, bracing himself against the wildly heaving deck as the E-boat flashed forward at full speed, opened fire.

That burst was tremendously frightening for Peter Egan. He ducked instinctively as a burst of glowing 20mm shells peppered the landing barge's superstructure. Ragged, steaming holes appeared everywhere as if by magic. The little radio mast came crashing down to the deck in a flurry of violet electric sparks. The coxswain groaned softly and crumpled to the steel plates, blood jetting from his abruptly shattered shoulder. Suddenly, startlingly, the power went. The steady chug-chug of the engine died away and the battered barge started to drift purposelessly.

"Torpedo to port!" someone yelled on Howling Mad's craft, its deck already savagely ripped up by a salvo of cannonfire, dead and dying lying everywhere in the bloody well of the barge.

"Fuck this for a game of soldiers!" Howling Mad cried above the terrible, frightening racket. He swung the craft round. It moved with ponderous, nerve-racking slowness. "Come on . . . come on, fuck you!" Howling Mad cried, the sweat streaming down his crimson face, his eyes bulging out of his head like those of a man demented.

Luck was on the commando officer's side. Just in time. The deadly weapon of war, packed with a ton and a half of high explosive, went hissing harmlessly by the hull with inches to spare. Next moment it was gone in a flurry of bubbles.

But that sudden turn had flung one of the grievously wounded over the side. Now he was floundering in the sea, weakly splashing the suddenly red-flushed water and crying piteously, "Give me a hand, mates . . . I'm going under . . . Give me a hand for God's sake!"

Egan didn't hesitate. He ripped off his helmet and webbing belt in one and the same moment. Then he plunged over the side into the freezing water the way he might have done back home in one of the lakes during a summer vacation. Ignoring the slugs cutting the air lethally just above his blond head, he struck out for the dying, drowning soldier.

"Oh, good show, that man!" Howling Mad exclaimed as he spotted the figure knifing through the waves in a professional crawl towards the drowning soldier. "Take his name for afterwards, Adj . . . if you can get it." Then he forgot Egan as the Adjutant grabbed for his pad and pencil. The E-boat had swept round in a tight turn, her mast seemingly touching the water, her wake flying upwards in white fury higher than the funnel. Now she was hurtling in once more, 20mm cannon blazing, as if to put every lumbering barge to the bottom of the English Channel.

That wasn't to be. As if by some miracle, a British Sea Fury of the Fleet Air Arm dropped out of the sullen sky. The pilot caught the E-boat skipper completely off guard. One moment he was concentrating on the kill, the next he was shrieking with pain and rage as his severed right arm dropped to the heaving deck in a great gob of crimson blood and he was on his knees, sobbing for breath.

The Sea Fury pilot showed no mercy. At mast-top height, he hosed the surprised motor torpedo launch with shot and shell. The Oerlikon gunner hung dead over his cannon. Masts came tumbling down. The bridgehouse lay suddenly in smoking ruins, dead and dying men packed together like lovers in a last passionate embrace.

Slowly, the abruptly powerless E-boat came drifting to a stop, white smoke pouring from its shattered engines, the shell-pocked craft already listing badly to port, while the terrified survivors threw Carley-type floats, rubber rafts, anything that would float overboard and prepared to spring after them before their boat went down.

Then the Fleet Air Arm pilot came round in a tight turn directly above the dying boat. "Oh, I say!" the commando Adjutant exclaimed in dismay. "He's going to shoot 'em up. Not cricket. The fellah's a bounder, sir!" He looked appealingly at Howling Mad.

"If he is, Adj," Howling Mad chortled with delight, as the pilot opened up once more at the crippled, helpless E-boat, "we need more of his kind. We'd win this friggin' war a darned sight more quickly."

Five minutes later the dying E-boat shuddered violently like a live thing seized by a sudden fever. What was left of her superstructure began to tumble in angry confusion to the body-littered deck. "The sod's going under!" the commando corporal cried. "That'll serve them Jerries right. Having a go at us like that."

Egan looked up from where he was attempting to tend to the wounds of the man he had rescued, packing great yellow-and-khaki shell dressings on the gaping wounds only to find that the bandages were soaked in his blood the very next moment. The man was dying; but still he tried.

He frowned. Suddenly he could feel no sense of triumph as a dead German sailor floated by the landing barge, the corpse bobbing up and down in the wavelets, its lifejacket keeping it still afloat. It all seemed so purposeless. Men who had never met before, never exchanged a cross word, men with similar worries and hopes. Yet they had attempted to kill each other mercilessly and without thought Abruptly he was sickened. It was all so wrong. He shrugged and then went back to his hopeless task. The man was obviously dying under his hands.

Across the way, Howling Mad O'Rourke felt no compassion. They were Huns, the enemy. It was his job to kill them. All the same he knew the commandos had failed. For a second time they had been shot up by enemy aircraft. It seemed almost as if they had a jinx on them.

The Adjutant seemed able to read his thoughts. He said, "Sir, I think somebody's going to get a bollocking for this one. Either the Navy or the Brylcreem boys have slipped. We should have had better protection."

"Just so," Howling Mad agreed. "Now let's get our skates on and head back to port. The sooner the sawbones start working on my poor lads, the better."

Half an hour later they entered a small Cornish harbour. Hastily the wounded were carried ashore through the surf on doors, chairs, anything that would support their weight. Then came the sodden secret papers in their weighted tarpaulin sacks. After them the dead, both British and German, lined up like so many pieces of driftwood on the chill, wet sand and covered hastily by blood-stained tarpaulins.

The weary commandos, their shoulders bent with fatigue, followed, with Howling Mad repeating mechanically to each one of them as they passed, "Good show, well done, lad!" All save Egan to whom he said, clapping him on the shoulder, "Very bravely done, Peter. There might be a gong in this for you. We'll see . . ." Then they were all gone, seeking the shelter of the little white-painted fishermen's cottages to the front, leaving the lonely dead to stiffen in the evening breeze. Higher still, Hard Man put away his stolen binoculars. He had seen enough. Now he knew he was right. Like some predatory wolf he stole off into the grey gloom. Moments later he had vanished altogether. Now the only moving things in that remote place were the winter trees in the icy wind.

Chapter Five

"Doctor Argent, of Dieppe Place, Barnet, was fined a total of ten pounds, plus three guineas costs yesterday, it was reported today. She had allowed precious bread to be wasted. As the prosecution stated she had ordered her charlady to throw bread to the birds in her garden. In her defence she told the court she could not allow the poor birds to starve in these hard times."

"Turn that bloody thing off!" Mountbatten snapped sharply, obviously in a bad temper.

As the officers shuffled to their feet on his entrance, they looked at each other significantly. Someone obviously was going to get a rocket.

The Home Service died a sudden death as Mountbatten, handsome face set and drawn, ordered, "Please sit down, gentlemen, and let's get on with this bloody awful business."

Mountbatten wasted no time. His anger obvious, he launched into an attack on the operation's senior officers, while O'Rourke smirked, obviously enjoying the brass's discomfiture. According to Mountbatten, the destroyer captains who had been supposed to protect the commandos' convoy knew as much about sea warfare as the "youngest snottie straight out of Dartmouth". As for the commandos, they had a lot to learn still. They had been "little better than an idle bunch of broken-down landlubbers."

At that, Howling Mad bristled and half-rose to his feet to protest, but Egan pulled him back in his seat before he could do so.

Finally a flushed Mountbatten ceased his harangue and looking at his officers grimly, said, "All right, so you made a complete balls-up of the exercise. *Splendid!*"

They looked up at him as if he had suddenly gone mad under the strain.

Mountbatten forced a wry smile. "Yes, you heard me correctly – splendid! I say that because you will have learned a lesson from that fiasco. You won't repeat the same mistakes a second time." He lowered his voice and added, half-jokingly, "Because if you do, you won't survive to a second rollocking from me, will you!"

Now it was their turn to smile, though Howling Mad looked as angry as ever. At his side, the 'young hero', as one of the destroyer captains had called him, wondered if his CO ever smiled.

"Problems?" Mountbatten went on, his face serious again. "Fortunately that Jerry E-boat was destroyed. Because we have secret information at the highest level, the source of which I cannot disclose to you, that the primary task of the Jerry was not really to shoot up the commando convoy." He paused significantly and then dropped his bombshell. "That Jerry E-boat was out to get a commando prisoner and whip him back to the Reich for interrogation."

The announcement caused consternation in the lecture hall, which belonged to the local Methodist church, and was currently decked out with naive, highly coloured watercolours obviously done by the children at the local council school. While he listened to the excited talk all around him, Peter Egan's mind wandered and he asked himself if one day those little children would ever find out what momentous events had occurred here. Somehow he doubted it. By then they would have all forgotten about the war.

"So it's pretty obvious," Mountbatten cut into the chatter roughly, "that Jerry is on to us one way or other. It's also obvious that by risking a precious E-boat to pick up a prisoner that the Jerries don't know all that much. That is something to be thankful for."

Howling Mad struck his huge fist into the palm of his other paw in exasperation. "Can't anything go bloody right for this op!" he exclaimed to no one in particular.

Mountbatten, ten yards away, must have heard the outburst but if he had he took no notice of it. Instead he said in a sombre voice, "That's not all our troubles." He clicked his fingers. "Call Captain Harkins," he snapped to an elegant aide, with his golden lanyard hanging from the shoulder of his immaculate uniform.

A moment later a middle-aged captain, wearing the medals of the Old War, limped a little uncertainly onto the stage, his artifical leg creaking audibly. He looked about him, obviously put out at the sight of so many important-looking, high-ranking officers.

Mountbatten looked at him winningly, obviously attempting to put him at his ease. "Captain Harkins," he explained, "is the intelligence officer at POW Camp 57, which holds mainly hard-nosed Nazi prisoners."

His audience absorbed the information with some bewilderment, obviously wondering what German POWs, however hard-nosed, had to do with the great attack on St Nazaire.

A moment later Harkins enlightened them. In that patient, careful, solicitor's voice of his, he said. "I know, gentlemen, that this is for the time being mere supposition on my part. But bear with me while I tell you the hard facts – and then give you my conclusions."

Peter Egan warmed to the 'retread', as they somewhat contemptuously called the men from the Old War called back to the service. He looked tired, but sincere: a man who wouldn't give up easily despite his years and failing health. His father of 'Hell's Last Issue', the Highland Light Infantry, had looked like that before he died.

"Two nights ago," Harkins began slowly, "we had a breakout at Camp 57. We soon put a stop to it." He grinned slightly and Egan guessed there had been some sort of fun and games that night which must have pleased the probably bored old 'retread'. "However, one prisoner *did* escape. And he was the most dangerous Hun of all. Hard Man, he is called, by both his fellow Huns and ourselves."

Mountbatten looked pointedly at his expensive gold wristwatch but obviously, Egan told himself, that cut no ice with the 'retread.' He was going to take as much time as he felt his explanation needed.

"So Hard Man got clean away," Harkins continued in that same slow, even pedantic manner of his. "It is obvious that he had a well-thought-out plan from the very start. How do I know that? I shall tell you, gentlemen." He leaned forward as if about to inform a client that a long-lost uncle had died and left him a goldmine in Australia. "Hard Man had been on the outside at least three times before his final escape. He changed uniforms with other rank POWs and went out on a working party. Now, if you know the ways of prisoners of war you must know that some will go to extreme lengths just to get away from their fellow POWs for a day or so, knowing that they are going to be recaptured soon. I suppose they're sick of barbed wire, the stink of unwashed male feet and the like . . ."

Egan told himself the old 'retread' was poking gentle fun at his listeners. They knew nothing at all about what would motivate a Jerry POW to do a bunk.

"However, our chap had three chances, at least, to get away for a few days or so. But he didn't take those chances. So," he paused significantly, "it is my guess, gentlemen, that he used those three outings to prepare for something more important than just a jaunt to enjoy the beauty of the English countryside or whatever my Jerry old lags long for on the outside."

Howling Mad looked puzzled. He ran his thick, sausage-like fingers through his thatch of flaming red hair and groaned, "That old boy has completely lost me, Egan. You, too?"

"A bit, sir," Egan admitted and leaned forward to hear better what the 'retread' on the platform was now saying.

"Now on one of those days outside, while dressed in the uniform of another German able seaman, our Hard Man happened to be at Southampton docks when you commando chaps returned from an exercise and were shot up in the anchorage by those damned Jerry tip-and-run raiders."

Suddenly Howling Mad looked interested. "I say," he said, "I see what you mean, Captain—"

"Shut up, Major," Mountbatten cut him short curtly. "Let Harkins get on with it, *please*. It might be something important he's got. . . . it might be not, too."

Harkins went on: "Well, gentlemen, as I understand it those commandos were on important exercises for some raid or other."

"You might as well know, Harkins, you've signed the Official Secrets Act. It's on the French port of St Nazaire."

"Thank you, sir. Well," Harkins continued, "could it be possible that Hard Man learned about that raid from one of the commandos? There were several wounded among them and some fatalities. You know what men are like when they are dying. Everything else is forgotten – family, service, country. All dying men are concerned with is themselves." He stated the matter as if it were a self-evident fact. It was the voice of a man who had seen a lot of his fellow men die painfully and violently in his time.

At Peter Egan's side, Howling Mad nodded his agreement. It was obvious he felt the 'retread' was right.

"If that is the case, gentlemen, and knowing Hard Man's temperament – he's a fanatical Nazi and patriot – he will do his utmost to get that vital information back to the Hun authorities, cost what it may. He has already betrayed a score of his comrades in the camp to make sure he could escape. I would put nothing past him now. *He won't hesitate to kill!* After all, according to his warped mentality, anything – and everything – is justified in the cause of Folk, Fatherland and Führer, as the National Socialist creed has it."

Suddenly, the old man staggered slightly and clutched his side, while his listeners talked among themselves, discussing the information. They didn't see the involuntary reflex, but Peter Egan did, as well as the abruptly opened mouth, slightly twisted to one side as if the 'retread' was fighting for air. He had seen such spasms often enough in his dying father before the war when the pain had made him gasp and choke, as if he were being strangled by an invisible pair of hands. With the certainty of a vision, Peter Egan knew that the 'retread' was dying on his feet; he wouldn't see another Christmas.

But Captain Harkins recovered with surprising alacrity. He tapped the side of the simple army trestle table, perhaps for attention, and said a trifle weakly, "Now I would like you gentlemen to keep your eyes open for Hard Man, especially you commandos. I have a description and picture which can be posted in the various messes – officers' and other ranks' – if you wish. But my guess is that you won't see him around here. He will now be concentrating on getting across the Channel by the shortest possible route, taking his information about you with him."

"Surely we can stop the damned fellow?" Mountbatten objected. "After all, we are on an island."

The old 'retread' didn't answer immediately. It was as if he were giving the question serious attention. Finally he spoke and what he had to say didn't altogether please Mountbatten, that was obvious. "In 1940," he replied, "at the time of Dunkirk, our whole sea-going nation was organised to get our boys back from Europe. You know all those chaps who muck about in boats and the would-be-yacht club commodores forgot their pleasure and got on with the job. Then came the threat of the invasion and they didn't object to having the boats registered, immobilised, tied up in secure berths. That was two years ago. The pressure is off now. People go horse-racing again. On every village green in the summer you can watch people in white flannels playing cricket while our boys get killed in North Africa," he added, his bitterness all too clear. "The vast majority of people have got used to the war and if they are civilians they are out for the good money they can make and the pleasure they can buy with that money—"

"Please hurry it up, Captain," Mountbatten snapped. "We haven't got all day, you know!"

"Yessir," the old man answered dutifully. "The point is, sir, that there are small boats at berths, very laxly supervised and with their engines filled with black market petrol, all along the South Coast. There for the taking by any bold, resourceful man." He shrugged, suddenly very weary. "It's going to be a devil of a job guarding all of them."

Mountbatten looked aghast at the tired old man. "You mean this – er – Hard Man of yours has got a good chance of getting away with the details of – er – you know what?"

Harkins shook his grizzled head. "He might think so, sir. But as long as I'm on his tail," he dropped his hand to the .38 fixed to his webbing belt, which dropped a little ludicruously on his skinny waist, and left the rest of his sentence unsaid. But they all knew without saying what he meant. The security briefing ended. But as they streamed out of the little Methodist church into the harsh winter sun, which made them blink, Howling Mad O'Rourke Said, "Peter, I like the cut of that old man's jib. If anyone can take this Hard Man fellah, it'll be him."

Peter Egan didn't answer. But as they passed the line of drab women, carrying wickerwork shopping baskets and waiting patiently outside the village butcher's with the legend in white on its window! 'Kidney or liver today.

Ration books A to H' he told himself that Howling Mad was right; but the old 'retread' would never survive to enjoy his triumph. For already he had the mark of death upon him . . .

Chapter Six

"Oh, it's reet luvverly," the Yorkshire sailor moaned with delight as she rubbed away with all her strength. He gripped the blackouted lamp-post as if he feared that she might tug him away from it with all that force and spoil his pleasure.

At the corner, her blacked-out torch at the ready, on the lookout for the rozzers – they were very active in the warren of streets with their 'condemned' houses around the docks – Clare turned and cast a glance back at her friend Chloe who was busy masturbating the merchant seaman just off a collier from the North.

She was all right; it was the 'client' who was doing the moaning. All the same Clare, the more practical of the two teenage runaways, told herself she'd better keep an eye on her long-term friend. Chloe was pretty, but not too bright in the head even though she had been to the local convent school, while she, Clare, had been fortunate to scrape through the eight 'standards' of the local board school. Once, Chloe had almost given it away to a bloke who had just been shipwrecked instead of demanding the usual ten bob 'for a good feel and a tight wank', as they described the services they offered their 'clients', always in advance. It was better that way, then the men didn't get no fancy ideas. Why, they'd even had an American

107

merchant seaman who had had the cheek to ask Chloe to do something nasty with her tongue. They hadn't even known what he meant at the time and had had to look it up in the medical dictionary at the local Newhaven library. "What a cheek!" Chloe, usually a very gentle person, had exploded, "asking a nice girl to do that kind of thing. But still what can yer expect from a *Yank*?"

At the lamp-post the man was saying thickly in between great sobs of breath, "I'll give yer a quid if yer give me a quick shag. I'm clean. I'll wear a french letter if yer want, Miss."

In the silence of the backstreet, broken only by the wail of some stray cat searching the ashtins and finding nothing, Clare heard the request quite clearly. Immediately she started to whistle her warning signal, *'Twas in an English garden . . .'*

Chloe heard it immediately and resorted to their usual tactic with a 'client', who was getting too pushy. "I think the bobbies are somewhere about. I haven't got time to take me – er – knicks off."

"All right," the sailor choked, obviously almost finished.

Already it was too late, for the sailor gave a sob, followed by a moan, muttering, "Oh, ferk the crows . . . I've gone an' ferkin' come!"

Chloe frowned. The nuns would have made him say 'Hail Marys' for a month of Sundays for cursing in that manner. "Watch yer manners," she warned, as he sagged against the lamp-post still moaning. Wordlessly she handed him the rag she kept for such purposes.

"Ta," he said weakly. "Ta very much." She waited till he had wiped himself clean, handed her back the rag together with the ten-shilling note. He staggered off into

108

the inky darkness without even a "Goodbye, be seeing yer." But as Clare always said, "There's only one thing men – the pigs – is after, Chloe, and when they've had it, all they can think about is fags and wallop."

Chloe waited till the northern seaman had vanished, then she hauled up her tight skirt to reveal her skinny naked thighs, the pink garters and the white virginal cotton panties beyond. Carefully she tucked the ten-shilling note inside the elastic of the knickers. As Clare, the practical one, always reminded her, "Yer can never be too careful, Chloe. Once I had a cheeky bugger – excuse me French – and when he'd had his wank he had the cheek to nick the ten-bob right out of me hand."

Using the torch Clare made her way across to the lamp-post where Chloe was spraying herself with that expensive perfume '*Soir de Paris*' that she used, although it cost the earth on the black market. "What d'yer think, Clare," she asked, "shall we go to the Regal? We haven't missed the main feature. It's Robert Taykor – ooh! I *do* love him, although he's a Yank, and—"

"You ready for a good time?" a harsh, accented voice cut in.

The two teenage whores turned, startled. Instinctively Clare flashed her torch in the direction of the sound. The blue light illuminated a doorway some five yards away. "Hey, you cheeky bugger," she exclaimed angrily. "Yer've been watching all the time. Don't yer know that was private!" She sniffed. "But some of you men have funny tastes. Are you some kind o' peeping Tom or some-at?"

She stopped short as she saw the speaker's face for the first time. It was hard and brutal and although the man was smiling his eyes didn't light up. They were cool and calculating, as if he were trying to assess them for reasons of his own.

Clare tugged Chloe's arm. "We'd better be off," she whispered, "I don't like the look on his ugly mug."

Chloe didn't allow herself to be pulled away. She said, "He's a big fellow. I bet he's well built."

Clare gasped. "Shame on yer!" she chided. Of late, her friend, convent-educated as she was, had begun to take an interest in sex. Giggling a lot she had whispered from behind her hand about the size of the men's 'thing', as she called it. Clare didn't like the new trend at all. Naturally they slept together in the shabby room they rented above the blitzed shop, mostly for the warmth (there was no heating), and a couple of times when Chloe had thought she had been asleep, her frail little hand had wandered under Clare's frayed vest and touched her loins. Clare hadn't mentioned it, but this new trend worried her. A girl could get herself into trouble if she started those games. She knew from her mother that if a man's 'thing' ever get close to you 'down there', yer could get in the 'family way'. It was the same if she didn't wipe the privy seat after a man had sat there. Besides, as her mother had hinted darkly, "Yer can get all sorts of 'orrible diseases as well if yer not careful. They say that some of them men-swine have their 'things' drop off from it." Now Chloe was obviously impressed by the stranger's size. It was disgusting, Clare told herself; she was thinking about size of his 'thing' on account of it.

"Like to put me up for the night, ladies?" the big man asked in an accent that Clare couldn't quite identify. "Won't be no bother. I – er – doss." Clare noticed the man seemed to hesitate over the use of the word, as if he were wondering whether it was the right one,

"On the damned floor, if you like. Mind you, ladies, I sleep with you as well, if you like, *Gottverdamme*" he cursed gutturally and Clare thought she recognised the accent now; she had had plenty of dealings with foreign sailors ever since she and Chloe had run away from Holloway to dodge being called up for the Services – "I can't see mesen in khaki bloomers, Chloe!" – or one of Bevan's great armanent factories that ran 24 hours a day, 7 days a week. Pulling men off was much easier and, even without ration cards, they always had money to buy whatever grub they wanted on the black market. There were spivs everywhere. "You Dutch?" she asked.

"*Ja, ja*, me Dutch," the big man answered swiftly. "Refugee. Back in 1940," and for good measure the man added a few words in what he thought was that language. "*Nix in Winkel, alles in Keller*," he touched his belly and then his loins to make his meaning quite clear.

"None o' that there 'ere!" Clare snapped. "No dirty talk with us. We're good girls, we are."

Again Chloe simpered but said nothing. Clare felt her long-time friend slipping from her grasp. These days, it seemed, her silly blonde head was full of men's nasty 'things'. "Well?" she demanded, as the man grinned down at them from the doorway in the unnatural blue light of the torch.

"Well, what?"

"What d'yer want to do, Chloe?" she snapped angrily, "about this here bloke." She jerked her thumb contemptuously in the man's direction.

"I've got money," the big man said. "Lots of money. Just been paid off till the next ship comes in to take us back to the East Coast" – he meant that of America; and everyone knew those who risked their lives on the

111

dangerous convoys from there were exceedingly well paid.

"He's lost his country," Chloe said, "to come here and fight for good old England."

"My arse! He's risked his life for the cash bonuses, that's what you mean."

"Now, miss," the man said carefully. "Don't be so hard on a poor sailorman. It's no fun out there in the Atlantic in all weathers—"

"Don't be rotten, Clare," Chloe said, trembling a little as if finding it hard to control herself. "I've made up my mind. He's coming with us. Oh, you are awful, Clare. Can't you see that the poor man needs a place to sleep for the night."

The big man looked suitably weary and in need of a good rest after the perils and hardships of the Atlantic crossing.

"All right," Clare said stubbornly. "Clever dick, where *is* he going to sleep? As you well know, we've only got the one bed."

Chloe laughed hollowly. "You're not that smart, Clare Raymond. There is the settee in the kitchen. I know the rats have been at it and the springs are none too good, but if you're tired you can sleep on a clothes line. So there." She cheekily stuck her little pink tongue out at her best friend. Clare could have slapped her at that moment, but she didn't. Instead she shrugged and said, "All right, have it your own way. But don't blame me." She switched off her torch with an air of finality.

In the sudden darkness, which had him blinking for a moment, Hard Man allowed himself a grin of triumph. He had done it just as he had planned. He had found himself a place, convenient for the beach and the small boats anchored there; a place where no questions would be asked. After all, he told himself airily, whores never asked any questions. All they ever bothered about, whatever their nationality, was *money*.

Moments later, 'linked up,' as she called it, to Chloe, he was on his way to their digs, followed by a sullen Clare, who was muttering to herself. Whether they were threats or not, Hard Man didn't care. *He* was in charge of the situation now. One more day and he would be on his way back to the Reich, bearing the all-important secret with him.

"You know," Hard Man ventured, as he lay there half-clothed on the horse-hair couch, with the rusty springs that squeaked every time he moved his big, muscular body, "you're showing the flag – *and it's black!*" he chuckled throatily, feeling that sudden thickening of his loins which he had almost forgotten about in ten months of sexless captivity.

"What?" she asked puzzled. She had felt she daren't use the tin bucket the girls kept for such purposes in the shabby bedroom; it made a devil of a noise when they did. He would have heard all right and in the morning she would have been ashamed to face him. So she had slipped out from beneath Clare's arm and, treading carefully as her friend continued to snore softly, she had crossed the icy floor in bare feet and headed for the privy in the backyard, where the toilet paper consisted of last week's *Empire News* cut into squares and stuck on a rusty nail next to the grimy wooden seat. She had been clad only in her skimpy, tattered vest, which barely reached the cheeks of her taut, girlish buttocks. But she had reasoned the big Dutchman would be fast asleep on the battered kitchen settee.

Now as she returned, the voice which had startled her, told her she had been wrong. Instinctively her arms flew upwards to hide her pink-tipped undersized breasts.

Again the man on the couch, his brawny, hairy chest uncovered despite the coldness of the kitchen, repeated his statement and chuckled.

"What . . . what do you mean?" she stuttered puzzled, *"Showing the flag – and it's black?"*

"Look behind you in the mirror. You can see by the light of the searchlights."

She turned her head, and gasped, flushing a bright crimson as she did so. Desperately she tried to pull down her skimpy vest to hide the patch of public hair displayed at her buttocks.

"They say that a black flag means surrender in some countries," he said, raising himself on one elbow. He was wearing only a pair of underpants and she couldn't take her eyes off the bulge at the front of them. It seemed to her to be tremendously big.

Chloe didn't know whether to feel ashamed at his words or giggle. Yet at the same time she felt a fascination for this man that she had not felt for any of her scores of clients in the past. They had been simply shadowy figures, concealed in doorways or bombed-out buildings, mumbling and panting, weak men who gave her nothing save money. This man was different. He was a real man, who looked at her not like some pleading sailor with a ten-bob note in his hand. This was a man, she knew that instinctively, who would *take* what he wanted – and at this moment, with her legs feeling like jelly and her skinny, virginal body trembling, she wanted

114

to be taken. Whatever Clare said to the contrary, it would have to come in the end; and this, she told herself with total conviction, was the man who should do the taking.

"Come closer," he said softly. "I won't hurt – if you don't want me to."

Mesmerised, she did as he commanded, watching herself, as it were, as she crossed to the settee on her bare feet; as if she were viewing some totally different person than herself.

He reached out his hand. She could see the muscles ripple the length of his naked arm. The hand touched her bare knee. It was hard and horny like that of a man who had been used to tough physical labour. She didn't mind. Indeed, she enjoyed the touch of that horny palm on her soft skin. Slowly he moved his fingers up her thigh. She didn't protest. She felt a thrilling tingle surge through her whole body. For a moment she felt she might wet herself with the almost overwhelming pleasure of it all.

He pressed her inner thigh, fixing her with that almost hypnotic look of his, his hard face revealing nothing. "Open your legs," he commanded quietly.

Obediently she did as she was ordered, not caring that she was revealing herself, Clare's warnings totally forgotten.

"Good," he said, his dark eyes glittering suddenly. He said something in a foreign language, which she didn't understand. It didn't matter. For he had now risen and she could see that impressive bulge had grown even more. She swallowed hard, her eyes fixed on it with an almost desperate longing. "You get on sofa," he said, his English very strange now.

115

She did so.

"Spread your legs."

Again she did as he commanded, not caring that she was revealing all her skinny, girlish nakedness to this man whom she had known for a matter of hours.

He wet his middle finger and slid it gently and slowly down between her legs.

She shivered as if in the grip of some raging fever.

"*Gut*," he sighed. "*Sehr gut!*"

She didn't understand but it didn't matter. All she wanted now was for him to do it to her. Her whole being was concentrated on that as her loins started to tremble as if of their own volition.

Slowly, very slowly, as her gaze followed the movement with dry-mouthed greediness, he started to slip down his underpants and that great column of taut flesh came into view, and her heart seemed to stop beating in a mixture of longing and fear. *Was he going to thrust that great hard roll of flesh into her?*

With a gasp of pleasure, he lowered his body onto hers. She felt something touch the entrance to her sex. She nearly died with the pleasure of it. It went in deeper. The pain was exquisite. Her spine arched with pain-pleasure. She bit her bottom lip to prevent herself crying out. He grunted and thrust deeper. The rusty springs of the broken-down settee groaned in protest and she could hold herself no longer. With the hot urine trickling down between her legs, she screamed.

"*Scheisse!*" he cursed as Clare came hurtling through the door to take in the scene

"You rotten pig!" Clare cried, taking in the scene, Chloe on the settee with her legs spread, the naked, muscular man, his face flushed crimson, and that great stiff roll of

116

flesh thrusting out from his hairy loins like a policeman's truncheon. "I'm going to call the police . . . *I'm going to have the law on*—"

They were the last words she was ever to utter.

Chapter Seven

The time for the great attack had almost arrived. In their camp just behind Falmouth, the commandos prepared, as outside in the harbour the naval force went about their practices, urged on by senior officers shouting at them irately through loud hailers.

Strangely enough for such a loud, wild man, Howling Mad O'Rourke had become quieter, almost paternal with his men now that the op was so close. He no longer flew into instant rages, letting off steam by bellowing at his commandos at the slightest mistake on their part. Instead he was gentle with his men, asking questions about their home life, whether they had written to their loved ones – 'just in case' – clapping them warmly on their shoulders, congratulating them when they performed well. It was almost, Egan told himself, as he accompanied the CO as orderly officer on his rounds, as if the CO knew that some of them were going to die soon and didn't want to add to their misery in their last hours before the inevitable happened.

That morning they paused at yet another group being lectured by a young commando officer, who was saying earnestly, "Keep the moon behind you, men. You can control your own shadow like that and merge with the other shadows. Watch out for fruit trees, even in winter. They usually harbour lots of bloody birds."

"Ones with two legs and skirts?" some wag asked.

There was laughter from the others, which under different circumstances Howling Mad would have quelled instantly with one of his tremendous roars. Now he smiled benignly and laughed himself.

"'Fraid not, Jenkins. Watch them all the same. Disturb the birds and they can make a bloody awful racket. A steady shuffling through the grass won't disturb, but the slightest scrape or click of metal – a bayonet or rifle sling jingling, that sort of thing – and they'll cause a terrible racket!"

Gently Howling Mad guided the young Canadian officer away towards another group being lectured to by an elderly white-haired civilian, who was maintaining, "No need for fancy footwork, lads. A good swift kick to the goolies and that'll settle his hash. Always been my experience – a kick in the balls, a boot stamped on the bugger's face and yer'll hear no more from that particular sentry!"

"Look at 'em," Howling Mad, his voice a mixture of pride and sentiment. "Before the war most of them were on the dole – thirty bob a week. Even in the Army, if they are just a private soldier, they don't earn much more. And here they are now, preparing perhaps even to die for a country that didn't do exactly its best for them while they were still alive." He nodded his big head with its flaming red hair, as if to confirm to himself that what he said was correct. "A good hunch, you won't find any better, Peter."

"Yes, sir," Egan heard himself say respectfully, while his mind took in the CO's words and he realised that the big major was not just 'piss and vinegar', as the latter

119

would have formulated it himself. The man had heart, despite his frightening appearance.

"Now, Peter," Howling Mad went on, more business-like. "You're a new boy so I'm not giving you an actual command on this one." He saw the look of sudden disappointment on the young Canadian's handsome face, and added hastily, "Don't worry, you're going to be blooded on this one, sooner or later, Peter. By the law of averages, one of my young troop officers is going to buy it on the raid. Till that happens you stick with me and the Adj, so that you're at my disposal at a moment's notice."

"You mean a sort of reserve of officers, sir?"

"Exactly – a *one-man* reserve of officers, that's all we've got. But I need you on the spot so I know *instantly* where to place you." He sighed a little and stared out across the grey-green sea to where the destroyers, trailing thick black smoke behind them, rehearsed a smokescreen. Perhaps he could see things out there, visible only to him, and they weren't pleasant. "All right," he said after a moment, "let's get back to the vehicle for a mug of tea. They're bringing up the tea and wads for the lads' break." In silence they walked across the windswept turf of the clifftop. Behind them the wizened old civilian was still advising gleefully, "A kick in the goollies, a boot stamped on the bugger's face and yer'll hear no more from that particular sentry . . ."

At his main HQ in Portsmouth, Mountbatten was also working flat out making the final preparations for the great assault from the sea. As he told his virtually exhausted staff, army and navy: "Winnie's breathing down my neck, *hard*. We can't allow anything to go wrong on this one. He needs it to impress Roosevelt and the American people." He allowed himself a weary smile. "If we do make a balls of it, it will undoubtedly be Iceland for the duration for us."

"And, yes," one of his staff whispered behind his hand to his neighbour. "There'll be no promotion or gong in it for our Dickie."

His neighbour allowed himself a weary laugh. They all knew just how much Mountbatten loved winning medals. It was said, perhaps maliciously, that he spent many a night when he was alone in his quarters fondling and admiring them.

But now the aristocratic commander had no time for such indulgences. He knew he was working against the clock, not only to get the preparations for the raid finished by the deadline set by Churchill, but also to beat the Germans. For it was quite clear by now that the enemy were on to them and were aware that the British were going to attack the coastline of Occupied Europe. It was just a matter of learning where and being prepared to repel them, hopefully with a great loss of life. For as London Intelligence had informed him the day before, "It's clear from the intercepts that we've been picking up – *by means of you-know-what**, that the Hun knows this is slated not only as a military victory, but also as a propaganda coup in order to impress the Yanks – and at this stage of the war, with the fighting reaching a critical stage for Germany in Russia. The last thing Hitler

---

* Intelligence was probably alluding to the top-secret ULTRA decoding operation on German Sigint being run from Bletchley Park in the Home Counties.

wants is Roosevelt joining the war against Germany on our side."

But while Mountbatten waited for further information from the middle-aged captain of Intelligence, Harkins, he dealt with the thousand and one matters to which he had to give his final approval. Nothing could be overlooked in what was soon to come; there would be no follow-up supply route.

How many blindfolds would they need to cover the eyes of the German prisoners they would probably take and bring back to the UK?

Should gas capes be provided in case the enemy used that most terrible of weapons.

Who should be provided with gold sovereigns, special secret escape maps, names and addresses of underground contacts for escape purposes – just officers or key personnel from the other ranks?

Time and time again Mountbatten felt like pulling his hair out with sheer exasperation as yet another query which apparently could be dealt with only by himself landed on his desk.

Now time was beginning to run out. Already the destroyers were loading supplies, rations, ammunition, medical stores and the commando landing barges were undergoing their final running tests before they were launched back into the sea for the great raid. By now the staff officers, wan, haggard, with deep circles of fatigue under their eyes, staggered around like sleepwalkers. Still Mountbatten drove them on relentlessly with "after they're off, chaps, you can sleep the clock round as far as I'm concerned. Then your job will have been done." But even as he said the words, he knew he was lying. None of them would be able to get a wink of sleep after the great assault convoy had sailed. The tension would be too great. It would be only after they had learned the outcome of the attack on St Nazaire that they would be able to relax and perhaps sleep at last.

It was about three on the last afternoon before the troops would march down to the docks to embark that Mountbatten was startled out of the routine of the boring paperwork by an excited aide-de-camp. "Sir!" he exclaimed, nearly forgetting to salute as he came into Mountbatten's great echoing office. "Sir!"

"Where's the fire, James?"

"It's the provost marshal at Newhaven, sir. He's on to something. He'd like to talk to you immediately."

Mountbatten frowned. He didn't like this sort of request. He had been brought up in the protocol of court. This was the wrong way, to his mind, for a lowly officer of the Military Police to approach a senior naval commander and an aristocrat to boot. "What did he say?" he asked testily, putting down his expensive silver fountain pen.

"Not much, sir, as far as I can gather. But it concerns that old boy, Captain Harkins, who spoke to us recently and the chap he was after. At all events, the bobby chap said it was of the utmost importance. Otherwise I would have dis—"

"Give me the phone," Mountbatten cut him short.

The aide handed him the phone and he listened attentively to the sudden flow of words at the other end in Newhaven, while the aide watched his chief's haughty, handsome face for some clue as to what was going on.

Finally, Mountbatten said, "I can't get to Newhaven myself, Captain. Pressure of work, but tell Captain Harkins he has *carte blanche*. He should take this fellow alive if he can, perhaps we can squeeze something out of him. But if

123

he can't," he shrugged carelessly, "he has my authority to get rid of the chap, no questions asked. The fewer people who know about it, the better. Is that clear?"

Apparently it was for Mountbatten put the phone down the next instant with an air of finality, his face revealing nothing as he picked up his fountain pen once more.

Opposite, the aide shivered involuntarily. For the first time he realised just how hard and cruel these senior commanders were. They signed men's lives away without even blinking an eyelid.

Chapter Eight

Harkins whistled softly as he viewed the scene from the bombed-out fish-and-chip shop opposite. The girl, her petticoat stained with blood, her legs spread in obscene invitation, lay dead on the wet cobbles. Not more than five yards away, sprawled in the grotesque posture of those done violently to death, was the Redcap corporal. His peaked cap had rolled into the gutter and the flap of his leather pistol-holster was open. Harkins reasoned that his pistol had vanished.

Next to him, the Provost Marshal for Newhaven, a heavy-set Londoner with a dark, smouldering un-English face, who looked like a former detective constable with the Met, confirmed the old Intelligence Officer's guess the next moment by snarling angrily through his gritted teeth, "The bastard had the sheer bloody nerve to come out and nick poor Charley's pistol afterwards. Ten years in the ruddy Smoke and I've never seen anything like it. That Jerry of yours must be a real hard-nosed villain."

"He is," Harkins said softly, sizing up the situation, his gaze flashing constantly to the blitzed house opposite where Hard Man and his female hostage were holed up. "He'll stop at nothing. He knows that if he's taken he's for it."

"Yer, the bastard deserves to do a last little jog at the

end of Pierrepoint's piece of hemp," the Provost Marshal said, referring to the public hangman, Albert Pierrepoint. "Mind you, he has got the girl, a poor, frightened little tart. Sez he'll barter her for a boat."

Harkins shook his grizzled head solemnly. "I'm afraid that's completely out of the question."

"He sez he'll do her in if he don't get the boat and free passage out of Newhaven."

Harkins frowned. He hesitated to say what he knew he must say, but it had to be expressed aloud so that the burly ex-dectective constable knew where he stood. "Then I'm afraid that she must die, poor girl. There are greater issues at stake."

"But she's barely eighteen, according to the records the local bobbies have on her."

"No matter," Harkins replied quietly. "We need him, that's what is important *now*."

"Alive?"

Harkins shrugged. "It doesn't matter which. Alive or dead. He's going to die anyway."

"Yer can say that again. Still that poor lass . . ."

"What's he got in the way of weapons?" Harkins interrupted him firmly, his mind full of other things.

"The knife he did that poor tart in with and Charley's duty pistol."

"How many rounds?"

"Five in the magazine and one up the spout, I suppose, and perhaps one or two mags in reserve attached to the outside of the holster."

"Perhaps eighteen in all."

"Something like that."

Harkins considered the information for a few moments. Down in the harbour the seagulls swept across the dirty, polluted water, calling mournfully. Hard Man, he told himself, would play it out to the end, but when he didn't get his way he would resort to that atavistic Hun fatalism. He wouldn't allow himself to be taken alive; there'd be shooting all right and other people would get hurt, perhaps fatally. Not that that would worry Hard Man. He would die happily, believing in some primitive heathen glory. Still he would give him one last chance. He turned to the Provost Marshal. "All right, I'm going to have one last go at the Jerry."

The policeman looked worried. "Take care, Captain. I wouldn't trust that fellah as far as I could throw him!"

"Don't worry. I don't either." Harkins took a deep breath and then stepped out from cover into the street that smelled of stale cat's urine and newly spilled blood. He looked up at the shattered upstairs window, the only one not boarded up in the shabby, blitzed house with a warning sign nailed to the door, announcing: 'No entry. Looters will be shot'. "*Sie . . . hören Sie mich?*" He held his hands up in the air to indicate he was not carrying a concealed weapon.

"*Ja, ich höre Sie, Herr Hauptmann,*" Hard Man replied. There was a sudden yell followed by a slap and a subdued whimper. Obviously he had struck the girl, his hostage. "*Was wollen Sie?*"

"For you to let the girl go and surrender. You haven't a chance!"

Hard Man laughed scornfully. "That's what you say. I've got the cunt." He mumbled something and for an instant Harkins caught a hurried glimpse of the hostage's terrified, ashen face in the cracked window before she was ordered to get down again. "You see. Let me go and she lives. Don't and she croaks it." Again the trapped man

127

laughed harshly. "So who's got the trump card now, *Herr Hauptmann?*"

Harkins didn't reply. There was no chance to. Suddenly the grey morning gloom was stabbed by angry scarlet. A slug whined off the wet cobbles in front of him in a shower of red and blue sparks. Hard Man laughed maliciously as Harkins dived for cover. "Not bad for an old man. You moved fast. Next time perhaps you won't."

The Provost Marshal crawled through the brick rubble to where Harkins sprawled. He noted automatically that the old man's liver-flecked right hand was trembling violently. Poor old sod, he said to himself, he's too long in the tooth for this sort of caper. Aloud he said, "You see, I told yer the Jerry sod was barmy. I don't think we're gonna get away with it. We'll have to give him what he wants. I can alert the patrol boats off the boom. They'll pick him up without trouble. Why take risks, Captain?"

Harkins forced himself to shake his head. He felt a little sick. It had been a close shave. "There's many a slip between cup and lip, as the saying has it. Let him get out of that house with some kind of free conduct to the harbour and a boat and you don't know how the bastard might turn the tables on us. No," he said gently but firmly, "he's not leaving that house!"

"It's your funeral, Captain."

"I hope not," Harkins answered. The feeling of nausea had been followed by that nagging pain in his right side. He told himself that it was going to be his funeral sooner or later anyway. He'd never see that boring old legal practice of his again, with its conveyances and wills and maiden ladies wasting hours of his time with their petty bequests to remote relatives. So what did it really matter? Best to go out in some kind of glory than wait for the inevitable which would be just as predictable and boring (though perhaps painful) as the months that had gone before it.

"If necessary," he broke the heavy, brooding silence, his voice crisp and authoritative like a man used to giving orders and having them obeyed, "you can give me covering fire, though I think it might not be necessary."

"How do you mean, Captain?"

"You see where the landmine landed which destroyed the houses all around, well that looks like dead ground to me, as far as the Hun up there is concerned. There's plenty of spill left over from where they filled in the crater."

"It take your point," the Provost Marshal agreed, without too much conviction. He knew from the ribbons on the other man's chest that he had to know about such things. All the same, he was old and slow. "Just one thing," he said carefully. "There's about five yards or so where there's no cover or dead ground just beyond that spill. You'd have to be pretty nifty on your feet there."

Harkins smiled slightly. "I know, but I'll manage it. I've done it before you know."

"*Yer*," a hard little voice at the back of the other man's mind snarled cynically, "*but then you were nearly a quarter of a century younger, old pal.*" Aloud he said nothing and watched as the Intelligence Officer took out his .38, took each of the brass bullets out in turn, gave every one a polish with his handkerchief to obviate any stoppage, replaced them and then swung the breech closed once more. He was ready for what was to come. He grinned and stood up and while the Provost Marshal stared up at him, wondering if he were seeing him alive for the last time.

Harkins mumbled the old, cynical doggerel of the

trenches just before an attack, "For what we are now about to receive may the Good Lord make us truly thankful." A moment later, without another word, he was stealing towards the dead ground afforded by the spill.

"What in three devils' names is the old fart-cannon up to?" Hard Man queried, a little puzzled as Harkins rose and then stole into the cover of the ruined building next to where the 'chained dogs'* were hiding.

Next to him, Chloe, her ashen face stained with tears, her vest torn, with dried blood caked to her naked inner thighs, looked at him.

"Wonder what he's about?" he said in English. He had enjoyed fucking her and he had felt more relaxed afterwards than he had done for many a month. But then the trouble had started once the other foul-mouthed harridan, her so-called friend, had burst screaming into the debris-littered kitchen.

Chloe remained silent, her face blank. There was no light in her eyes. Obviously she was in shock.

Hard Man looked at her, as if seeing her for the very first time. "You liked it, didn't you?" he demanded. He chuckled evilly. "One day when you've got kids – one of them might even be mine – you can tell them you were fucked first by a *Hun*," he emphasised the word maliciously. "I wonder what they'll say to that?"

She gave no response.

"Did you not hear?" he snapped, eyes blazing suddenly.

* German Army slang for military policemen, due in the German Army to the plate of office, attached to a chain which hung from their necks while on duty.

130

"Are you an idiot or something? *Ach dumme Pfotze,*" he cursed in German and then in an abrupt rage he thrust the muzzle of his pistol close to her ashen face. "Say you liked it, cow!" he threatened.

A faint light appeared in her eyes, as if she were only vaguely aware of what was going on. "What?" she stuttered.

He thrust the muzzle into the side of her skinny cheek until she yelped with pain. He repeated his question, clicking off the safety. "*Well?*"

"Yes . . . yes . . . I liked it!" she stuttered in sudden terror.

"I filled you up with it, didn't I! You enjoyed that Hun salami filling you up." He felt a sudden sexual urge and pushed the long hardness of the muzzle deeper into her cheek, "Say!"

"*Yes . . . yes . . .*" she stammered hurriedly.

"I—" He stopped abruptly. He had heard something move close by; like a stone being dislodged. He forgot the terrified amateur whore at once then pulled the pistol away and turned swiftly to the dirty, shattered window. He peered out, keeping low, just in case they had brought up a sharpshooter to pop him off. The English were a treacherous, wicked race. He wouldn't put anything past them. They might even kill the girl in their attempt to get him and then blame him for her death later. The English – they were like that.

Nothing . . . nothing moved out there. All the same he knew he had heard something. Carefully he looked, going over the ground metre by metre as he had once done on the bridge of his U-boat, searching the heaving horizon for some new unsuspecting victrim, finger around the trigger of the heavy pistol. Still he saw nothing. He relaxed a

131

little. Perhaps it had been one of the many rats or the stray cats which scavenged the bomb ruins in their dozens.

Suddenly Hard Man felt he had had enough. The Tommies had had enough time to make their decision about him. He raised his pistol, knowing that he was going to waste a precious round, but knowing, too, he needed to attract their attention. He poked the big pistol through the shattered window and yelled, "I give you another 30 minutes – *then she dies.*"

Next moment he pressed the trigger. The noise echoed and re-echoed around the ruins, as close to him the girl jerked violently with shock. Nothing happened. The houses opposite remained stubbornly silent. It was as if he were the last man alive in the world.

But in his hiding place, Captain Harkins nodded his approval. Now the Hun had exactly 16 rounds left.

Chapter Nine

"*Junger Herr*", his dying father had always addressed him as "young sir", as he sat there with the rug over his wasted knees in the strange basketlike carriage in which they wheeled him around. It was usually just before *Abendbrot* – supper – when the morphine had eased his father's acute pain that he had spoken to the little boy in his Wilhelmian old-fashioned sailor's suit, with the cheerless, cold room growing dark (no fires or light before 1800 hours his father had always insisted with his parsimonious, Prussian self-denial). And always it had been a lesson in discipline and sacrifice.

When his father had come home, pronounced incurable, from the naval hospital, to find Kiel's mutinous sailors going on a rampage, throwing their officers overboard from the fleet, tearing off their medals and badges of rank, it had completely soured his already dour personality. Now after raging at the politicians of the new Weimar Republic – "those Red swine who stabbed our soldiers in France in the back" – he would pronounce on his son's future. "It will not always be like this, *Junger Herr*," he would rasp in his drug-and-schnapps-thickened voice. "We Germans are not meant to be losers, the running dogs of the victorious powers in the West. We have a destiny to fulfill," and when he had uttered those words his eyes

133

would flash for a moment, his claw-like hands gripping the sides of the basketwork chair would grow white with effort and suppressed rage. "But to regain our rightful place in Europe, perhaps in the world, we must learn to fight once more, not accepting life tamely as something that has been decreed for us by fate. We good Germans must never give in, do you understand that, *Junger Herr? Never give in!*" and he had fixed the little boy in his short blue trousers with that terrible gaze which had frightened so many sailors when he had held sway on the quarterdeck of his pre-war Dreadnought.

It was a lesson that Hard Man had borne with him for all his life. It had echoed and re-echoed down the dark recesses of his mind when he had fought the communists in the great street battles of the 1920s; in those dreadful years as an ordinary seaman on a training schooner, rounding Cape Horn, soaked to the skin day after day, living off a revolting mixture of stale bread and cold porridge; right up to his first fighting cruise of the war when his U-boat had been badly shot up, so much so that they had been unable to submerge and had limped home, bombed and machine-gunned by the enemy all the time until finally they had entered Kiel harbour: a death ship with dead and dying men lying everywhere in the shattered wreck of the submarine.

Now, as he crouched there next to the sobbing girl, he thought of that dour old man, his father, who even when he had been dying thought of one thing only: service to the Fatherland and duty. For some reason tears welled up into his eyes at the thought of the old man lecturing him in that freezing, darkened room, knowing that his life was ebbing away by the minute, but still not able to give up on his beloved Germany.

134

* * *

In the town next to the quay, a weary old clock started to chime the quarter. Hard Man jerked his head back and shook it a couple of times like a man trying to waken from a deep sleep. Next to him, the girl stopped snivelling and looked alarmed. He knew why. She was sensible enough to realise that he would shoot her in cold blood if his demands were not met. And there were still 15 minutes left.

He cupped his free hand around his mouth and, keeping low just in case the Tommies had brought up a sniper in the intervening period, he called, "One quarter of an hour to go. Make up your minds soon, *gentlemen,*" he sneered at the word, "or else . . ."

"Bastard!" In his hiding place, Harkins cursed at the ultimatum. He knew now that there was no turning back. He had to do it, and do it before it was too late. Again a wave of nausea swept through his skinny frame and for an instant he thought he might have to vomit. Then it passed and he forced a weary grin. "You haven't got much to lose, old man," he told himself almost happily, for some reason he couldn't fathom, a smile on his wrinkled face. It would be hard on his wife. But she could sell the practice and she would get a war widow's pension. Beside she had made her private peace with the world the day that buff telegram had arrived from the War Office, the message starting with those fatal words, '*The Adjutant General regrets to inform you . . .*' Her life had really ended that day, too. She wouldn't survive him for long.

He forgot everything save the job at hand, slapping his pocket into which he had slipped the pistol. Sometimes holsters jammed and he knew he had to be quick to deal with Hard Man, who was half his age and whose reflexes were much faster.

Wasting no more time, he uncocked the pistol and started forward, crouching low as if he were back in 1916 on the Somme, setting out on some desperate trench raid when the motto had been 'Kill or be killed'. Carefully he skirted the spill left over from filling the landmine crater. He paused, gasping a little with the unaccustomed exertion. He cocked his head to one side and listened hard. Nothing. He took a deep breath. Now he was going to have to cover the five yards of the bombed street that was not in dead ground. *'Move it or lose it'* – those hard-nosed bastards of training instructors back at the base at Etaples in France had always used the slogan as they had entered the 'bullring' for bayonet practice. He grinned. At this moment he had no intention of losing it.

He clicked the safety off his pistol, flashed a quick look to left and right and then up at the cracked window of the room in which Hard Man was holding out. He started forward, heart beating furiously as if it might burst out of his rib cage. There was no sound save the wail of a ship's siren down below. The world, it seemed, had gone to sleep. But Harkins knew that wasn't the case. There was sudden death awaiting him if he put one foot wrong.

He slammed into the wall opposite. He had done it without being spotted. To his immediate front there was a door. It hung from its hinges, looking as if it hadn't been painted since the now-ruined house had been built. He leant there for a few moments, getting his breath back. He reasoned the door led through the passage to the outside earthern privies in the house's communal yard. It was just what he required. It would obviate making a frontal assault, which would be to Hard Man's advantage, who would be quicker on the draw than he, Harkins. He pushed the rusting metal handle. Nothing happened. The door was jammed 'Damnation!' he cursed soundlessly and squeezing his fingers through the gap, heaved. The door moved, the hinges squeaked noisily. Up above, Hard Man raised himself and chanced a look outside. Something was going on. But what?

The Provost Marshal caught a quick glimpse of his face before the German ducked behind cover once more. He, too, reacted seizing the loudhailer and bellowing "Give yourself up, man. We're bringing up the troops." Hard Man fired. The Provost Marshal reeled back into the debris, blood jetting suddenly from his right shoulder in a bright red arc. The loudhailer tumbled from his abruptly nerveless fingers.

But the noise the loudhailer had made covered the sound being made by a somewhat frantic Harkins as he forced the door open and entered the passage that stank of sweat, ancient lecheries and despair. On tip-toe he moved down the dark, stone-flagged alley, his nostrils already assailed by the stench of human ordure from the privies at the back of the yard, their doors long vanished.

He passed into the house itself. That was easy. The back door had long vanished like those of the privies. Obviously someone had stolen them for firewood; coal had long been unobtainable in this part of the world.

Inside it was dark and he had to move more cautiously. The floor was covered with rubbish and brick debris. He might stumble and make some noise which would immediately alert the trapped man above him and the Hun wouldn't hesitate to fire straight down through the lathes of the ceiling, now devoid of plaster. He wouldn't have a chance.

So Harkins took his time. He felt the sweat begin to trickle unpleasantly down the small of his back. He tried to ignore it. He had other things, life-or-death things, on his mind now.

He approached the wooden stairs cautiously. A couple of pictures hung lopsidedly on the wall, the glass shattered. He saw they were trembling slightly with the vibration from just above his head. Was Hard Man moving about? Had he twigged?

Suddenly, startlingly, it happened. With great savagery, a fusillade of angry fire sprayed the air all around him. The Hun had spotted him. He loosed off two slugs and then the bullet hit him in the arm with a blow that sent him staggering backwards. It felt as if a red-hot poker had been plunged savagely into his flesh. In spite of himself he yelled out in acute pain. Next moment he tumbled to the steps.

There was a loud echoing silence, which seemed to go on for ever. Abruptly there was a soft footfall. Lying there, helpless for a moment or two, Harkins heard it quite clearly. "Hard Man," he whispered aloud.

He pulled himself together and fumbled hastily for his pistol, the palms of his hands lathered with sweat in his urgency. The German was coming down to kill him!

The door at the top of the stairs creaked open.

There stood Hard Man. He took in the scene immediately, seeing the man lying bleeding on the debris-covered stairs, good hand searching for the pistol a few inches away. He chuckled evilly. "Hard cheese, as you say, old man." He raised his pistol to administer the *coup de grace*. "End of the journey for—"

He never finished the sentence. A nearly nude girl

threw herself at Hard Man, who went staggering back. Automatically he pressed the trigger of his pistol. Bullets peppered the ceiling above him. Whitewash floated down like flakes of snow as he reeled and fell under the impact of that flying body. But he didn't lose his grip on his pistol.

Harkins knew his luck was running out. He had only one chance left. Already he was beginning to feel dizzy through loss of blood. Everything wavered and trembled in front of his eyes. A red veil of unconsciousness threatened to overcome him at any moment. "Get back . . . get back, girl," he commanded thickly, blood trickling from the side of his mouth. The girl rolled to one side as Harkins seized his pistol.

Hard Man was quicker. He recovered from the surprise attack almost immediately. "Die, you bastard," he choked with rage, his face, crimson, *"DIE!"* He pressed the trigger, eyes gleaming with angry triumph. Click! Nothing happened.

Harkins didn't give him a second chance. In the same moment that a frantic Hard Man removed the stoppage and fired, Harkins did the same. The bullet ploughed right into the centre of the German's guts. He was lifted from his feet, pistol tumbling from his big fingers as his stomach shattered, splattering the stairs with gobs of crimson blood and gore. "Hun," he whispered fervently, as if it was part of some holy creed. "Hun . . ." His head tilted to one side like that of someone too weary to carry on, while Hawkins, dying as he lay splumped there in a pool of his own blood, blinked, closed, opened and closed his eyes for good.

It was like that that the wounded Provost Marshal found them. The dead German slumped in a stinking

139

heap, the sobbing, nearly naked girl and the dead Captain of Intelligence his mouth gaping.

For what seemed a long time the Provost Marshal could not speak. Then as the urgent jingle of an ambulance came from outside and there was the rush of heavy boots, he crossed himself with difficulty and whispered, as if to himself, "May God rest their poor souls . . . *all* of them!"

BOOK THREE

END RUN

Chapter One

"Unidentified object off the port bow!" the cockney lookout sang out unexpectedly, as they ploughed steadily through the sluggish grey-green sea at 0700 hrs.

As one, on the bridge of the Hunt-class destroyer HMS *Tynedale*, Commander R.E.O. Ryder and Colonel A.C. Newman, leader of the commando raiding party, swung up their glasses.

It was the afternoon of the second day since they had sailed from Falmouth at 1400 hrs on 26 March. So far the little convoy of destroyers and motor torpedo launches, which now carried Newman's commandos, had encountered nothing more serious than the swell. On the bridge and stripped for action, the senior officers wondered as they focussed their glasses if they had run into the expected trouble at last. The long shape sliding noiselessly into the calibrated eye-piece of Ryder's glasses told the naval officer they had. "Damn and blast!" he cursed, for there was no mistaking the object to their port bow, "A Hun U-boat!"

Almost immediately there was controlled chaos. The klaxons began to shriek their warning. Sailors pelted along the slick decks, scrambling into their flash gear and helmets. Others flung themselves behind their guns. An excited young sub began to shout "Bearing red three-oh

. . . range 5000 yards . . . deflection zero. *SHOOT* . . . *SHOOT . . . SHOOT!"*

The gunners needed no urging. It wasn't often that they had such a soft target as this. Their 4.5-in guns slammed into action. Suddenly the deck was flooded with the acrid, choking smell of burned cordite. In a frantic chatter, the Oerlikons and machine-guns joined in. Tracer zipped lethally across the water. Great spouts of wild white water mushroomed up on both sides of the U-boat. But she bore a charmed life; nothing hit her.

On the bridge, an exasperated Commander Ryder slammed his clenched fist into the bulkhead. "Come on . . . for Chrissake!" he cursed, *"Sink the Hun sod!"*

It wasn't to be. The Germans reacted almost immediately. Dark figures scrambled up the ladder of the dripping conning tower. Faintly they could make out the wail of the German alarm signals. The last German sailor threw himself inside the conning tower and the hatch was slammed shut. White water, filled with exploding bubbles of compressed air, swept the length of the submarine's hull. At a terribly steep angle, the U-boat's bow disappeared beneath the surface in a wild crash-dive. Angrily, Ryder bellowed, knowing that he had lost her, *"CEASE FIRING . . . CEASE FIRING . . . PREPARE TO DEPTH CHARGE!"*

Together the destroyer and her sister ship surged forward. At 30 knots they swept towards their vanished target, a great white bone in their teeth. Behind them they left the slower *Campbeltown*. In two wild yet graceful curves they came in to depth-charge. At the sterns of the two ships, great round drums rolled over the side with huge splashes. Seconds later the creamy wake of the two ships erupted furiously. Water spouted 100ft into the air. Hastily

144

Ryder focused his glasses but nothing materialised. There was no sign of the vanished U-boat. "Bring her about," he yelled at the coxswain, "Let's go and have a look-see."

"Ay, ay, sir." The petty officer brought the destroyer round effortlessly and at speed; he knew, too, just how vital it was for the success of the operation that they must sink the sub, which at this very moment might be back on the surface and signalling their position to German Naval HQ.

Tynedale moved forward at a mere 10 knots. Ryder knew just how dangerous that was. The destroyer was a sitting duck for any determined U-boat commander. He could hardly miss at that slow speed.

While he waited, Ryder surveyed the surface of the sea for signs indicating that the sub had been hit: the usual flotsam and jetsam of floating wreckage and an ever-widening oil slick. There was nothing. In the end the two destroyer captains gave up and a worried Colonel Newman, sucking his unlit pipe as usual, asked: "Did you get her, do you think?"

Ryder looked angry. He snorted, "I don't damn well know, Colonel. That's the trouble with sea warfare. There are so many imponderables."

Newman took his pipe out of his mouth slowly. "Well, Ryder," he had to ask the question, now they had been spotted, "do we go on?"

Ryder knew well what the burly, mustached Colonel meant. At this very moment, that U-boat skipper might be alerting every German-held port right along the French coast; there could be a warm welcome waiting for them at St Nazaire. 'Operation Chariot', as the great assault had been named, might well end in a pitiless and bloody massacre.

Ryder considered carefully. What if he called off the op when in reality he had sunk the German sub? There would be one hell of a scandal back home. Heads would roll, especially after the *Scharnhorst and Gneisenau* scandal. Besides, if the *Tirpitz* did get loose in the North Atlantic because they failed to put St Nazaire out of commission, the vital food supplies from the US might well dry up in a few weeks and there would be no other alternative for Churchill but to surrender. He made up his mind. In a voice that was completely devoid of emotion, he said, "We go on, Colonel."

"Good show, Commander!" Newman answered in the same unemotional manner. He started to suck his old pipe once more.

At exactly 2200 hrs on the night of 27 March 1942, eight hours later, Lt. A.R. Green, in charge of the convoy's navigation, spotted the light rhythmically winking in the silver, moonlit darkness. It was the sign he had been tensely waiting for for the last hour. Hastily he summoned the Captain to the bridge. "It's the *Sturgeon*, sir," he said. He referred to the submarine which Mountbatten had ordered to act as a signal beacon off the mouth of the Loire.

Ryder beamed. "Fine job of navigation, Green!" he said enthusiastically, "Right on time . . . right on the exact spot!"

Green blushed.

Five minutes taken the submarine submerged, its task completed. All was haste in the convoy. Swiftly, Newman shook hands with Ryder as he and his staff transfered to the command launch which would direct the commando.

In the meantime, while the destroyers stood by, the assault prepared to move in. With it was the *Campbeltown*, two of

146

her funnels cropped to a low rake to resemble a German destroyer, two others removed, the black and white flag of the *kriegsmarine* of Nazi Germany flying from her mast. It was a legimate trick of war. Even if it hadn't been, no one would have cared that fateful night. The mission was too important.

Slowly they started to move towards the blacked-out port. There was no turning back now . . .

Howling Mad O'Rourke buckled on his claymore and checked if his bow was fixed firmly across his brawny shoulders. At any other time Egan would have chuckled at such an impossible CO, but not now. Everything was too tense as they headed for their objective under the cold spectral light of the moon.

Five minutes later, two white fringes like low cloud suddenly emerged from the silver gloom on both sides of the commandos' launch. "It's allright, Peter," Howling Mad hastily reassured his subordinate. "It's just surf. We're entering the mouth of the river."

Behind them a commando sang tonelessly an obscene version of 'Little Miss Muffet'.

"Put a sock in it, Jenkins!" Howling Mad cut in. "Can't hear myself think with that racket!"

"Sorry, sir," the crestfallen commando said and went back to cleaning his nails with the point of a bayonet, doing so delicately, as if he were in some high-class Mayfair salon.

Up ahead, the RAF were beginning to arrive on schedule. They were to provide the feint, deadening the noise the motor-launches made. "Here come the the Brylcreem boys," Howling Mad commented scornfully. "Let's hope their aim is better than normal. Otherwise we're going to get a nasty headache."

The bombers, 60 twin-engined Whitleys and Wellingtons, droned on as everywhere along the shore the German searchlights sprang up with startling suddennes. Their icy white fingers began to scour the clouds in search of the British planes. Moments later red tracer zipped upwards like a swarm of angry hornets. The bombers came on. Their flares parachuted down slowly. The bombing was about to commence. Howling Mad flashed a glance at his wristwatch. Eleven o'clock. They were dead on time. Everything was going splendidly. So far there hadn't been a single hitch. "Good show," he muttered.

The launch began to slow down. "What is it?" Peter asked.

"The mud flats, Peter. We've been informed about them. They'll slow us down. Hope that old tub the *Campbeltown* will be able to get across them. Her displacement is six times ours. If she doesn't, we'll be right up the bloody creek without a bloody paddle."

Peter Egan prayed that the ex-USS *Buchanan*, a First World War destroyer would not get stuck. Suddenly he gave a sharp intake of breath. The *Campbeltown* had shuddered visibly. Still she came on, the game old ship was making ten knots. She was doing it! The old destroyer shuddered once more. She had hit the mudflats again. Again she came on. Minutes later she was picking up speed and had crossed the last natural obstacle. Now there was nothing to stop them, save the Germans, a suddenly apprehensive Egan told himself with an abrupt chill of fear.

The German searchlights blinded them. Five minutes had passed. On the bridge of the MTB, her skipper shaded his eyes against the glare. He tensed as he waited for the enemy shells soon to come. But they were prepared.

They would trick their way in to the very last moment, if possible.

On the *Campbeltown*, Commander Beattie ordered Leading Seaman Pivex, "Flags, signal in German, 'Wait, don't open fire'." He added a captured secret German call sign. Hastily the signaller clicked and clacked his Aldis lamp.

The ruse worked so far. The searchlights died a sudden death. They were in darkness again. So far an enemy gun had not fired at them and they were getting ever closer.

Another five minutes passed in tense expectation. Soon the assault force would come level with the enemy's heaviest guns along the mole. A violent light. A crack and a sound like a huge piece of canvas being ripped apart. Next instant a shell whistled harmlessly across the water, towing a fiery, scarlet trail behind it.

"The fun and games have started," Howling Mad breathed. Next to him Egan tensed, as if he half expected a physical blow at any moment.

Again the assault force used a ruse. It signalled. "Cease firing – friendly force." And again the trick worked. The guns fell silent. "Christ!" Howling Mad commented, "They must be a bunch of brainless idiots." They sailed on.

Ten minutes later. Now they were in sight of the objective: the 35ft high steel sliding lock gates of the *Forme Écluse*. As Commander Beattie tensed on his bridge, Howling Mad shouted above the urgent throb of the engines, "Stand by lads! Soon be there! We're coming!"

"Ay," Jenkins muttered dourly to no one in particular, "Like friggin' Christmas is coming."

The seconds slipped by. The *Campbeltown* started to quiver dangerously as she gathered for the final act of her long sea-going life. The crew tensed, gripping stanchions ready for the shock of the collision. "Haul down the swastika – Up the White Ensign!" Beattie sang out telling himself that the old tub would escape the final ignominy of the breaker's yard. She would end in a burst of glory. When other ships would be long forgotten, *Campeltown* would still be remembered. As the rating ran up the White Ensign, German shells started to hit the old tub in real earnest. Time and time again she staggered under the impact. In a matter of moments the superstructure was smashed into a shambles and her 12 pdr and mortars were destroyed. Seamen began to fall screaming as huge pieces of red-hot, gleaming shrapnel scythed her decks in wild, lethal fury. Angry cherry-red fires broke out everywhere. But the outline of warehouses and sheds, which they had all memorised time and time again in training, began to loom up ever closer. They were nearly there.

Beattie yelled out the order! "Stand by to ram!" The engine-room responded beautifully. The old destroyer, damaged mortally, half the men on her dead or wounded, started to pick up speed. At 20 knots, the bullet-riddled White Ensign flying proudly from her one remaining mast, *Campbeltown* pierced an anti-torpedo net, then slammed into the dock gate. For a second more she continued her crazy progress. Her bow crumpled like a squashed banana. With one last great shudder she came to a halt, her screws churning the water into a white froth. Below the waterline the sea started to pour through the great holes rent in her hull. HMS *Campbeltown* had fulfilled her purpose.

It was exactly 1034 hrs. The *Campbeltown* had destroyed the main sliding gate to the *Forme Écluse*. Laughing like madmen, the survivors, navy and army, began to clamber over the side onto the debris-littered quay, lit by the lurid red glow of the burning warehouses, to tackle the German gun batteries.

Operation Chariot was well underway.

Chapter Two

Cautiously Peter Egan raised himself to his knees, ignoring the mayhem and death all around. It was a mere ten minutes since the commando had landed and already Howling Mad's reserve of officers – himself – was exhausted, due to the initial casualties. Now at last, after three years of waiting, he had an active command – what was left of a troop – under his leadership; and suddenly he felt a little lost and helpless.

He was soaked with the flying spume. That didn't worry him. His problem was what to do next as he eyed the lines of dannert wire and a half-dozen pillboxes guarding the entrance to the channel leading to where the four German Moewe-class destroyers were anchored.

For the time being this section seemed strangely quite. Perhaps the Germans were too occupied elsewhere. For a fleeting instant he felt that he was going to die this cold morning, in a country he had never seen before. Then he dismissed the thought as nonsense, swearing at the same time he wasn't going to make a fool of himself. Behind him his men, all older than he was, waited for his orders. Their fates now depended upon his making the right decision.

"All right, lads, follow me," he commanded and was surprised to hear just how steady his voice was. He started forward for the dripping, green-encrusted concrete wall. He tensed. Nothing happened. The Jerries in their pillboxes had still not spotted the intruders in their midst. "Cutters!" he hissed.

The commando who had been singing the dirty ditty about Miss Muffet doubled forward. He handed the officer the heavy-duty wire cutters. Egan threw himself on his back. Lying full length with the wire above him, as he had been trained to do, he grunted, hands bleeding already from the cruel barbs, and began to severe the nearest strands. They parted with what seemed to him a hell of a racket. But still the defenders didn't react. He crawled through hastily, knowing that they were sitting ducks at the wire; his men crawled after him. "Prepare to move quick," he whispered, when they were all through. "Pass it on." He eyed his front. The warehouse to his immediate right was still shrouded in black silence. Their luck was holding out.

"Move it!" he hised urgently.

In that instant it happened. A soft, dry crack. A sudden hush. Next moment a flare hurried into the sky to explode in a fierce red glare, outlining everything below. Their luck had run out.

"Bollocks!" someone cried in the same moment that hoarse cries in German sounded the alarm. Almost immediately the German machine-guns fired, pouring a tremendous but inaccurate volume of fire to the front. It seemed as if they were confronted by a solid wall of lethal white tracer.

Higgins, at 29, was the troop's oldest man. The others joked and made comments about his false teeth and thinning hair, but he reacted first. "Try this on fer size, yer jerry buggers!" he cried. He swung his arm back like a bowler at a village cricket match and hurled the grenade towards the nearest machine-gun. Then a burst of enemy fire ripped the length of his upturned arm. He fell screaming, gobs of blood and torn flesh falling from the arm in a red rain.

Suddenly the machine-gun stopped firing.

Egan didn't wait for a second invitation. "At the double, lads. *In like friggin' Errol Flynn!*"

Laughing and crying almost hysterically, his men surged forward, weapons at the ready. A half-dressed German popped out of an underground tunnel and the look on his surprised face was almost comical. A commando, hardly pausing, or so it seemed, let him have a cruel burst from his tommy-gun. The man's face disappeared in a red blur like a soft-boiled egg cracked by too heavy a spoon.

They slammed into another wall. The Germans concentrated their fire on the obstacle. They knew the commandos would have to cross it. But first came the tangle of rusting wire. Egan, however, didn't even have to give an order. A commando slung his rifle. He ran full tilt at the wire. Next instant he was impaled on it like some khaki-clad Christ, bullets cutting the air all around him. Two other commandos pelted after him and flung themselves on the commando's body. Like a bridge of human flesh, they clambered up him and onto the wall. The others followed suit. Behind, they left the dying commando. Mentally, a gasping, sweating Egan made a note to find out the man's identity. He deserved a gong for his bravery.

They pelted forward, tossing grenades to left and right, heading for the cover of the warehouses. The night was crazy with the angry snap-and-crack of the fire

154

fight; grenades exploding with a throaty, thick crump; the thunder of the guns the harsh cries, the moans of the dying.

Egan ignored it, carried away by the crazy unreasoning madness of battle. He skidded to a stop at the corner of the nearest warehouse, heart thundering, breath coming in great hectic, excited gasps.

He heard the sound of smashing glass. He knew what that meant. Only the Germans could be inside the warehouse. They were breaking the windows to secure their field of fire. He didn't want to give them that chance to get entrenched. "Inside, lads and watch it! Winkle the buggers out before they settle in."

In haste, one commando bumped into another, with the classic lines from the BBC's *ITMA*, "After you, Claud . . . No, after *you*, Cecil!"

Then they were inside the big gloomy warehouse, snapping off shots to left and right, with Germans screaming shrilly as they slammed to the floor like bundles of wet rags.

Almost immediately, surprised by this sudden attack, the heart went out of the German defenders. They started to throw their weapons away, raising their hands and crying fearfully, "*Kamerad . . . no shoot!*"

"Christ!" a commando yelled in triumph, "they're pissing themselves!"

"We're going through 'em like shit through a goose," another joined in joyfully.

They pushed on, hardly noticing just how weary they were all becoming. Out in the fiery night there were flames everywhere. Up ahead lay the sleek outline of the Moewe-class destroyers with their sharp, sawn-off, rakish funnels. They were approaching their real objective, though as

155

Howling Mad had told them back in Falmouth, "Even the commandos can't tackle four 1000-ton Jerry destroyers. But we can make the crews go to ground while our own chaps do their bit." At that moment, Peter Egan prayed his crazy CO was right.

A hiss. What looked like an arrow hissed through the air only yards in front of him. On the roof of a warehouse opposite, a man screamed and came tumbling into the angry red light transfixed by an arrow that protruded from the small of his back.

"Watch your bloody back, Peter," a familiar fruity voice exhorted.

Egan gave a sigh of relief as the huge red-headed figure in the flying kilt emerged from the shadows, great longbow at the ready. It was Howling Mad. "How are we doing, sir?" Egan cried above the racket.

"Fair to bloody middling," the CO chortled. "Come on. No time to stand here like a couple o' dizzy housewives gossiping. *Move it!*"

With alacrity, they 'moved it'!

Now the Germans had marked them exactly. Accurate, heavy fire poured their way. The commandos started to take casualties, serious ones. Men went down in heaps, a confusion of heavy boots, flailing limbs, falling weapons. "Keep going, lads," Howling Mad yelled, trying to ignore the slaughter. A German with a stick grenade popped around a corner and attempted to throw it. To no avail, for Howling Mad's claymore sliced the air. The German's head, complete with helmet, tumbled to the wet cobbles and rolled away into the gutter like a football. And still they were taking casualties.

Another corner. The first of the German destroyers came into view. The crew were running back and forth excitedly. Bells jingled. Officers bellowed orders. Already there was the muted rumble of powerful engines being started up.

"Hold the bus—" a commando began and next monent fell to the ground, his body like a bloody sieve, through which his bright red life-fluid jetted.

They ran on, firing from the hip as they did so. Ragged fire met them.

"Bring up the two-inch mortar," Howling Mad yelled urgently, "That'll put salt on the buggers' tails." While he waited for the two-man crew to set up their tube and ready the bombs, he pulled an arrow from the quiver on his back, then threaded it against the taut longbow and fired the next instant. On the bridge of the German destroyer, a monocled officer looked in startled surprise at the arrow now protruding from his right shoulder, as if he were wondering how it got there. Next moment the monocle popped out of his eye and he fell back out of sight.

Almost immediately after that the little mortar tube belched. An obscene pop and stonk and the first flight of bombs were winging their way towards the still-anchored destroyer.

Wildly the crew scattered, as the mortar bombs came falling out of the sky with a vicious hiss. "Not much cop!" Howling Mad gasped, drawing out another arrow, as his commandos hesitated momentarily, waiting to brave the ship's fire, "but they'll put the wind up the Jerries for a few minutes."

He was right. As the bombs started to explode the length of the deck in little bursts of angry, yellow-red flame and smoke, the crew held their fire. They were too afraid to put their heads above the bulwark, because the commandos were picking off those who dared with unerring accuracy.

Another salvo of mortar bombs struck the Moewe-class destroyer. A couple of crewmen reeled back screaming, clutching shattered limbs. But the small 4lb bombs had made no impression at all on the destroyer's deck. Peter Egan bit his bottom lip with frustration. Time was running out rapidly. He could hear angry cries and gruff orders in German on all sides. The enemy had recovered from his first surprise. He was closing in on the hundred or so surviving commandos, who were trying to destroy the port installations and they were making little progress in their attempts to sink the German destroyer and block the channel.

Howling Mad seemed to read his thoughts, for he cried, "Fuck this for a game of soldiers! We're getting nowhere like this, Peter."

"What are we going to do?"

"See that tender or lighter or whatever it is." He indicated the dark outline of a much smaller vessel to the rear of the anchored destroyers. Its captain was frantically trying to get his ship out of the range of the commandos' fire.

There was the flash of another salvo of the little mortar bombs exploding and Peter, catching sight of the sharpnel-riddled flag at her bow, cried, "But it's French, sir!"

"Bugger that," Howling Mad snorted impatiently. "If those Frogs are working for the Huns, then I officially declare them honorary Huns, ours for the taking. Now that lighter is easy meat even for our two-inch. Knock the sod out and we'll have blocked the channel for the time being at least. Those Hun destroyers won't be able to attack our chaps heading back for Blighty. Got it?"

"Got it, sir," Egan answered eagerly. They'd soon finish the French lighter off and then they could see about getting back home. He flashed a look at his watch. There was another six hours till then. But by first light they had to be on their way before the German net closed around them – and they were taking casualties all the time. Already, he guessed rapidly, they had lost half their effectives; they couldn't go on like this much longer. He snapped out a swift order.

The mortar crew reacted immediately. They started pumping the rest of their bombs at the 'neutral' French ship. As the first of them came swishing dolefully out of the night sky, the French seamen didn't wait to be ordered to abandon ship. In panic, jostling and pushing each other in the lurid light of the already burning, shattered lighter's superstructure, they clambered or dived over the side into the oil-scummed water. "Good show!" Howling Mad chortled over the racket and pulled out his last arrow. "Shows the treacherous bastards what they get for working with the enemy." He threaded the arrow and pulled the string of the great English longbow taut. He might well have been one of his ancestors at Agincourt 400 years before.

He aimed. "Try that on—" Howling Mad's cry of delight ended abruptly. It was changed into a cry of painful surprise. Slowly, very slowly, the bow started to slip from his nerveless fingers. His knees started to give way.

"Sir . . . sir!" Peter Egan cried urgently. "What—" he stopped short. A great red patch was beginning to spread across the front of the huge major's battle blouse. He had been badly hit.

A hundred yards away the lighter began to go under

in a rush of escaping steam and great bubbles of air exploding on the surface. Then Howling Mad, too, went down for good.

"*Sir!*" Peter Egan overcame his shocked dismay. Hurriedly he ripped the camouflaged netting off his helmet and pulled off the yellow-and-khaki shell dressing that had been jammed under its cover.

Weakly, Howling Mad shook his head to indicate that he refused to be bandaged up.

"But sir . . ."

"Don't bother, Peter. I've been hit twice before in other shows," he gasped. "Then I knew, for all the pain, that I had a chance. Not now. Don't waste—"

The tremendous roar of the lighter's boilers exploding drowned the rest of the words. Peter ducked hastily as pieces of metal rained down upon them, holding his body protectively over that of his dying CO.

"Get 'em out now, Peter," Howling Mad gasped weakly, his eyelashes fluttering rapidly: a sure sign of impeding death, though Peter didn't know it. But he would, all too soon.

"We'll get you out, sir," he said, with more confidence than he felt.

"No you won't, Peter," Howling Mad whispered. His voice was getting very faint now, as if he was very tired and longed to sleep. "I'd only be a hindrance."

"But we've got to get out before first light. Then the Jerries'll start rounding up the last of us. I think they've already started." He indicated in the direction of the lockgate and HMS *Campeltown*. There the firing had almost ceased. "Now's the time."

With an effort, Howling Mad shook his head as he lay on the blood-stained cobbles of the quay, not even noticing the bursts of angry fire coming from the nearest destroyer. "The trick in this business is to do the unexpected. The Huns will be expecting us—" he coughed thickly, his once powerful body racked with pain, a thin trickle of black blood dribbling from the side of his slack mouth. "But we don't do them that favour. Once it's first light and after, they'll think what's left of us not captured will have done a bunk. They'll relax their guard." He coughed again, a strange rattle came from deep down in his throat.

Peter looked down at him in alarm. "Don't speak any more, sir," he pleaded.

Howling Mad shook his head with a trace of his former determination. Behind the two officers what was left of the troops was pulling back. The men were obviously still in good heart, Peter noted automatically. They weren't making a run for it in panic. Instead they backed, fired, backed off again and fired once more. He told himself they were making the Jerries pay for every foot of ground they gained. "Once the Huns think we've had it, they'll down tools. They're squaddies, too, aren't they? They'll have a spit-and-a-draw, go on a bit of looting. See if they can find any beer to sup. You and the rest of the survivors will be forgotten."

Peter Egan nodded his understanding, telling himself at the same time they had to get moving. They wouldn't be able to hold this position much longer. Already his perimeter line was a mere 25 yards away and German slugs were thwacking dangerously into the burning buildings all around them. It was only a matter of minutes before the survivors would have to make one last desperate run for it if they were going to have a chance of surviving. "Sir," he said, a note of desperation in his voice now, "there's no more time to discuss—" He stopped short.

Howling Mad had given a thick, unpleasant-sounding cough. His spine arched. He tried to say something. Then a great gob of dark blood welled from his gaping mouth and splattered onto the cobbles, and the body lolled to one side like a broken doll. Peter Egan knew there was no use taking the CO's pulse. He was dead. He leaned forward and gently closed the dead man's eyes with hands that were blood-stained and scratched from the barbed wire. In a voice that he hardly recognised as his own he commanded, "All right, lads, pull back. Break off the action . . . *pull back everywhere.*"

Minutes later they were filtering back to the alleys and evil-smelling narrow streets of the old port on the run, with every man's hand against them, leaving the German sailors still firing pointlessly into the glowing darknes. They had perhaps only hours to live.

Chapter Three

It was now nearly three in the morning, over an hour or so since HMS *Campbeltown* had smashed into the lock gate at the *Forme Écluse*. That had been successful, but the secondary operation, the commando raid, under the leadership of big, burly Colonel Newman wasn't going so well. The bridgehead he had intended to establish from which raiding parties could sally forth to destroy German installations hadn't materialised. Now his command was scattered hopelessly and his own party was under constant attack, with German infantry probing their defences all the time, they were under constant enemy pressure as the Germans looked for weak points.

Weary, face blackened, but still sucking his unlit pipe, the big, burly commando officer tried to sort out the confusion. To no avail, no sooner had he established a rough-and-ready CP when two German 88mms went into action with a frightening boom and a roar. The great shells ripped the night apart. Almost immediately Newman's party started to suffer casualties.

An old sweat of an NCO volunteered to tackle the great cannon with a tiny 2in mortar. Newman was too flabbergasted by the offer to object. The wizened little noncom, with his tattoos and permanently suntanned face from years of serving in India and Egypt, snapped

163

into action at once. His first bomb landed right on top of the nearest 88mm. Its gunners, a mess of flailing, gory limbs, went flying over their concrete emplacement. As a severed German head complete with coal scuttle helmet rolled to a halt in front of the jubilant NCO's feet, the gun ceased firing.

The noncom wasted no time. Once the German machine-guns centered in on him, he knew, "We've had our chips, lads," as he had told his men. They had the second gun under fire immediately. Again the NCO's little party struck lucky. The second burst of tiny 2in mortar bombs landed directly under the long barrel of the 88. They exploded immediately on a four-second fuse and the 88mm's long barrel drooped in submission like the head of a beaten dinosaur. "Luvverly fuckin' grub!" the little NCO exclaimed jubilantly. "All right, lads, let's fuckin' hoof it."

They needed no urging and 'hoofed it' while they were still in the land of the living, which wouldn't be long for most of them. For the time being, Newman's party was safe.

Again the burly Colonel sent out his demolition parties, looking for targets of opportunity. They surged into that crazy maelstrom of flame, fury and sudden death, while an officer and two NCOs attempted to find out what had happened to the rest of the dispersed commando. For a short while the bomb teams struck lucky. One party, Lt Chant and four sergeants, blew the steel door off a pumping station Hurriedly they pelted down the stairs into the interior, which stank of diesel and human sweat. They planted their time pencils 40ft inside the depths of the station. Knowing that they had only a matter of seconds before the time pencils detonated the rest of the high explosive, they pelted to the surface. They reached the top just as most of the station went flying into the burning sky. But not all of it. Frantic and disappointed, they found some sledge-hammers and with tracer cutting the air lethally all around them, went to work on the surviving installations like a bunch of demented navvies who had suddenly gone stark mad.

But already fate was beginning to catch up with the Newman party once more.

Urged on by fanatical young officers, armed with Schmeisser machine-pistols and crying hoarsely, *"Alles fur Deutschland . . . Tot dem Feind!"* the enemy infantry began to close in on the commandos once again.

Newman knew there was no use attempting to fight them off. This time it was a full fighting retreat. After all he had only 70 men, most of them wounded, out of his original force of some 300. Covered by some last-ditch volunteers who lay in the smoking brick rubble, calmly and deliberately picking off the bold young officers who were exposing themselves to danger in their efforts to urge their reluctant infantry on into the attack, he started to pull back to a safer rallying point.

They made it falling back with the Germans behind them, the snap-and-crack of the small-arms battle getting fainter and fainter as the volunteers died their lone deaths in the rubble, each man a hero whose exploits would never be recorded.

Finally, Newman ordered his men to squat in the shadow of a still intact warehouse, which had not yet been targeted by the German search parties, though undoubtedly it would be soon. For a few minutes they were safe, but not for long, he knew that.

Ignoring the time-pencil explosions, the crackle of rifle

fire, the roar and belch of flame from the German guns firing on the escaping navy ships, Colonel Newman took the pipe from his lips and gave his final orders: "Lads, you've done well, more than I could have expected from you. But now the party's over and it's time for Cinderella to go home."

There was some weary laughter at this, but not much. While they listened, the wounded pulled their blood-stained shell-dressings tighter and others filled their magazines with the last of their ammunition. Newman was pleased with the sight. They were not going to give up, he could see that. He waited till the roar of some ammunition dump going up inside the Old Port died down before stating without pathos: "This is where we walk home, lads. Our boats have been destroyed or have gone back without us. So we walk."

His announcement was met by excited chatter. None of his men wanted to surrender. They all wanted to carry on; *they* were not going to be taken prisoner and spend the rest of the war in a cage behind barbed wire.

"What about getting down to the quayside, sir?" someone suggested, "Then swimming upstream till we're clear of the friggin' Jerries?" Another said: "We could nick one of them Jerry tugs, sir, and run her down the Loire. We could head east, right into the Jerries. They wouldn't expect that. With a bit o'luck and the old commando spirit – bash on regardless, you know, sir – we'd be right through the toe-rags like a dose of Epsom salts before they knew what had hit the fuckers."

Newman smiled despite his weariness and the danger of the situation in which they found themselves. He shook his head. "No, lads, I worked it all out back at Falmouth. We're going to break up into small parties of four, each one with an officer or NCO leading. Then we set off for the Spanish frontier. I know that Franco's lot hate our guts, but we've got a route going over the mountains. Once we reach Barcelona – that's in the north – we contact the British consulate. Our chaps there will do the rest." He said the words with more confidence than he felt.

"Luvverly grub," someone said, "Think of all that Dago crackling. They say they're real hot stuff between the sheets."

"Forget the Spanish señoritas," Newman said. "Remember we're not going to surrender to old Jerry. If you bump into him, fight it out till all your ammo's gone. "He smiled at them suddenly, taking in those tough, unshaven faces that he had known now for two long years and which were somehow closer to him at this moment than those of his own family. "All right," he rose to his feet with a grunt, "let's make tracks. It's a lovely night for a long walk, isn't it!" Then they were gone into the glowing darkness, dark, doomed figures who would never see England again.

Those last words were the beginning of the end for No. 2 Commando.

An ugly six-wheeled German armoured car, its turret down, came rolling slowly down the narrow old road, its machine-gun swinging from side to side menacingly like the snout of some predator seeking its prey.

"Bollocks!" someone cursed softly. "It ain't fair, sending that ruddy great monster after us."

"What did you expect?" another of the hiding commandos mattered, "friggin' tea and biscuits and friggin' finger bowls?"

"Shut up!" Egan snapped. Already he was getting used to commanding men even when they were hardened veterans of battle and several years older than he. He sized up the situation, just as the German's turret machine-gun began spitting angry fire. Slugs howled off the bricks in a rain of splintered dust. Men howled, went down, some of them wounded for a second time. At a slower rate of fire the commandos' Bren guns took up the challenge, their bullets uselessly zinging off the armoured car's thick metal hide.

In a minute the armoured car would roll over their positions. But then, by a strange quirk of fate, the Germans themselves solved the problem, temporarily. Out of nowhere a German motorcycle, complete with sidecar, came howling out of a side street, right in the path of the armoured car. Its driver braked hurriedly and the turret gunner ceased firing; he didn't want to hit his own people.

A commando sergeant didn't wait for orders. He doubled into the debris-littered, smoking street. He knelt, gasping for breath and then brought up his tommy-gun. Next instant he let the motorcycle driver have a full mag. At that range the commando couldn't miss.

The driver was catapulted from his seat and the sidecar smashed crazily into a gas lantern. The post buckled like a length of soft toffee. Almost immediately the escaping gas ignited with a whoosh. A great jet of lurid red flame seared into the night like blowtorch. It spread, the heat making them shield their faces hurriedly. Hastily the driver of the armoured car, seeing the road ahead blocked, and the intense heat turning the steel plates a dull, glowing purple, reversed.

That was good enough for the fugitives. They were not giving the Germans time to find an alternative route past the gas jet. They turned and pelted into the darkness once more, the noise of their heavy hobnail boots reverberating in the stone chasms of the streets.

Time passed. They ran and ran, their hearts beating furiously, the breath coming in great asthmatic gasps. But the Germans seemed everywhere. Time and time again, the commandos were forced to turn at the sight of more German troops and fled down another road, followed by the angry, unaimed fire of the enemy patrols. Egan, by now almost at the end of his tether, realized that he was responsible not just for his own safety but for that of the handful of his remaining men, and that they were in a trap from which there was no escape.

But their luck was beginning to change, though for the moment the hard-pressed fugitives didn't know that. They had just knocked out yet another German machine-gun post and were fleeing down a relatively quiet street, hugging the shadows cast by the walls of the old houses, when there was a hissed exclamation from one of the ornate 18th century doorways. They froze.

There it was again, but this time it was followed by a couple of words in French.

Egan swallowed and tried desperately to remember his high school French. There it was again, "*Par ici!*" That meant 'this way', didn't it, he said to himself. Behind him the old sweat with the suntanned face hissed, "A Frog, what's he want?"

"It's a woman," Egan said.

"A tart? What's she up to in the middle of a friggin' battle?"

Next moment he found out. A middle-aged woman, with a shawl flung over her head and smelling strongly of cheap scent, detached herself from the shadows, approached the two commandos and to Egan's great surprise, threw herself at him and gave him a great hug, driving the breath from his tired body. "What . . . what?" he gasped.

169

"*Madame Bogex*," she answered happily, "*du bordell communal de Vieux Port*".

Egan couldn't follow the rapid flow of French. The woman beamed at him winningly and made a gesture indicating that she was willing to lead him somewhere, but to where? A harsh voice at the back of his brain said 'Caution!' Was it a trap? To sell him to the Germans?

"What's the old Frog on about?" one of his commandos asked in bewilderment, as if officers always knew everything, including the French language.

"I don't know, corporal," he stuttered. "She's speaking too fast for me."

The Frenchwoman seemed to read his mind and understood his hesitation. As the cries in German grew closer, with a harsh voice bellowing repeatedly, "*Die Tommies mussen hier in der Gegen sein . . . Los Manner*," she made a circle with the thumb and forefinger of her scarlet-tipped right hand and smirking wickedly but encouragingly as if she had made the gesture many times before to hesitant young men, poked the stiff middle finger of her other hand back and forth into the circle of flesh.

Still Egan looked puzzled.

Behind him the permanently tanned little sergeant laughed and cried above the shouts of the advancing Germans seeking them, "Well, I'll go to our bloody house!"

"What is it, Sarge?" a young commando asked.

"What is it!" the old sergeant exploded. "Are you still friggin' wet behind the lugs?"

"How do you mean?" Egan interjected, as puzzled as the young commando had just been.

"Why, sir, she's inviting us to hide in her place."

"And what kind of place is that?"

170

"Nothing less," the sergeant laughed, grinning, *"than a friggin' knocking shop!"*

"Christ All-fuckin'-mighty!" the young commando exclaimed, "What a way to friggin' well die . . . !"

Chapter Four

"We're poor little lambs what's gone astray, baa, baa, bas," one of the more seriously wounded, high on morphia, had chortled at the sight of 'les girls', as Madam called them, with their sleep-tousled hair, pulling out their steel curlers and tugging at their knickers, ready for action even now in the middle of the night.

"I know," the wizened, nut-brown old sweat of a sergeant had attempted to soothe the drug-high soldier, "I know. *Gentlemen matelots all are we, doomed from here to eternity . . . God have mercy on such as we –* Now then," his voice had become brisk and businesslike, "be a good commando and put a sock in it, private. Half the friggin' German Army's out there looking for us."

Dutifully the wounded commando had lapsed into a happy silence, busy watching a fat whore, with rolls of blubbber running down her yellow stomach, as she lifted her torn petticoat and with a sleepy yawn began to scratch her ample pubic hair. "Christ Almighty!" he breathed in astonished wonder at the sight, "a bloke could die happy in a place like this."

They certainly could have. By now they had been re-bandaged by the willing if unskilled whores, urged on by an impatient madam who had now changed from her shabby flannel dressing gown into a bright black silk dress which seemed to be her working clothes. It appeared that the whores, ranging from a raddled, middle-aged woman to skinny, teenage peasant girls with still fresh and innocent faces, had run out of bandages. For now the wounded sported remnants of black silk knickers tied around their wounds and laddered stockings so that, as the wizened sergeant expressed, "They look a proper shower . . . a real Fred Karno's, sir."

Peter Egan, drinking the first French cognac he had ever tasted, was forced to agree with him, though he hadn't the foggiest idea what 'Fred Karno's Army' was. Not that it mattered. They were under cover. The girls were obviously on their side and apart from distant bursts of machine-gun fire, with now and again the sudden shock of one of the commandos' time-pencils exploding, the enemy seemed to have left their immediate area.

Egan took his gaze off an elderly whore who had opened her legs to reveal her nakedness in open invitation, grinning at him with her toothless smile, and said, "What now, Sergeant Hands, what's the drill?"

The wizened sergeant, who had seemingly taken charge for the time being as if he were well accustomed to 'knocking shops', as he called them, grinned, "Well, sir, there is worse places to hole up for a couple of hours, you'll agree."

Egan nodded, blushing fiercely, as the elderly whore opposite wet her middle finger and ran it slowly and provocatively down between the sparse greying pubic hair. "I suppose you're right, Sergeant."

"Course I am, sir," Hands said cheerfully. "Cheer the lads up no end after what they've been through. Wine, and a bit of the other." He winked knowingly "If yer get my meaning, sir."

Egan looked up at him aghast. "You can't mean—"

"Why not, sir?" Hands cut in. He'd already marked the elderly whore for himself. At that age and with that mug, she'd be only too willing to please. Very obliging indeed.

"But what if the enemy came?"

Hands laughed easily. "Cor ferk a duck, sir. This little lot," he indicated the whores, who were laughing and giggling and already beginning their little tricks with the wounded lying on the floor of the '*Salon*', "would frighten the pants off'n any Jerry. They'd go out backwards, I'll be bound, sir."

And Peter Egan had been forced to agree. "So what's the drill?" he asked, trying to be military and official in the middle of these bizarre surroundings in the dead of night.

"Stay here till about first light. Let the Jerries bugger off for their grub, and we make a break for it at, say, 0700 hours while they're feeding their fat faces at the trough and the Frog workers haven't started for work. I was here in 1940," Sergeant Hands added. "The Frogs'll be in their bars knocking back the old wallop till 0800 hours before they set off to graft – if the Frogs ever do graft," he added scornfully. "So with a bit of luck, we'll have an hour when the streets is pretty empty and we'll have a chance to clear the Old Port."

Egan considered for a moment. Opposite, the elderly whore had placed her middle finger in between her toothless lips and was sucking it like some happy child might do with a lollipop.

Hands beamed and thought, "Luvverly grub! What a filthy race the Frogs are!"

"All right," Peter said, his mind made up. "We'll do it

174

as you suggest, Sergeant Hands." He flashed a look at his watch, noting as he did so that the glass was cracked. He'd been lucky there, he told himself automatically. "Four hours to go. Tell the chaps to get their weapons ready. Then we'll try to rustle up some grub. They've still got their iron rations. After that they can get their heads down for an hour. Post sentries."

The little wizened NCO looked at the young, fresh-faced officer almost pityingly. "Have a heart, sir!" he said.

"What?"

"Tain't every day, sir, that the lads get a whole whore-house to them-sens. I mean, once, after the Quetta quake of '35 in India, I went on leave in Bombay and hired a whole knocking shop with the money I'd nicked from dead wogs." He sighed. "Happy days. But most of them lads," he looked at the commandos in their tattered, stained khaki, most of them wounded, the weariness and overwhelming shock of battle etched on their young faces, "They'll never get another chance like this. All that beaver to be parted with tender, loving care." He laughed fondly. "Why, they'll be still thinking o' this night when they're grandads and their choppers is gone and they ain't even got the strength to bash their Hamptons." His face grew serious again. "Them that survives, that is."

Egan relented. "Of course, you're right, Sergeant Hands. Give them two hours and that's it. No boozing, mind you!"

"No boozing, sir," Hands echoed happily, the problem solved, it seemed. "They'll remain as pure as the driven slush."

"That'll be the day," Egan replied somewhat wearily, as if all this decision-making was a little too much for him.

175

Then Sergeant Hands was off to pass on the good news. "Lads, there'll be grumble and grunt for the next two hours, for them of yer that ain't nancy boys, that is!"

Egan sighed.

Half an hour later Peter Egan, his mind still in a jumbled whirl, for he was now reliving his first taste of action, lay fully clothed, save for his muddy boots, on Madam's own bed. *"Pauvre gentleman anglais,"* she had announced proudly, leading him to the over-furnished room with its pornographic pictures on the wall and smelling of ancient perversions. Obviously she thought he should not be present while the common soldiers took their rough pleasures, listening to the joyful sounds all about him: the rhythmic squeak of rusty bedsprings, the hectic gasping, as if a great race was being run, the grunts of pleasure – once even what sounded like a horse neighing. Somehow he felt a little blue, sad, cut off. He supposed it was because he was an officer and gentleman, who was not supposed to share the rough pleasures of the common soldiers. "Get away, buddy," a harsh voice at the back of his brain snarled contemptuously, "It's just ya wanta get ya rocks off and don't know how."

Ruefully he told himself that the harsh voice might well be right. For his sexual experience had been quite limited for a soldier who was now approaching 21. There had been the raddled seaman's whore at the port-of-embarkation, who had cried, "Hurry up, soldier boy. This is fucking freezing Halifax, ya know, not ya fucking Bermuda!" He had been glad enough to get it over with in a few minutes, pay her her five dollars and vanish hastily into the freezing, foggy darkness of the port area.

Thereafter, there had been nothing until he had taken up with a VAD nurse of genteel background. It had taken

176

weeks before she had opened her blouse after what had seemed hours, perhaps even days of persuasion, and had allowed him to fondle – "*carefully*" – her underdeveloped breasts, keeping a tight restrain on his breathing ("I don't like that sort of thing. It's so vulgar, don't you think so, Peter?"). Weeks had passed and she had touched his erect member hesitantly, as if it might have been red-hot (which it was, but not in the manner she imagined). Thereafter she had masturbated him a couple of times in the fields outside the camp, looking away demurely while she had done so, whispering shamefaced afterwards, "What must you *think* of me?". Six months after that, she had began talking about their engagement, "Now that I've given myself to you, Peter". He had been glad to flee to the commandos.

Now listening to his men enjoying themselves whole-heartedly and without inhibition, he felt the first stirrings of lust. Gosh, he told himself, how he wished he wasn't wearing the single pip of a second lieutenant, which cut him off from the rest. It was at that moment that a discreet, gentle knock at the door made him forget instantly the class-and-rank problems occasioned by that brown, Bakelite star. "*Qui?*" he said, knowing instinctively that it wasn't Sergeant Hands.

He was right. It wasn't. It was the Madam, beaming all over her plump, normally rapacious face with cash registers for eyes. She was pushing a poorly dressed girl in front of her, who didn't look a day over 15. The Madam looked from left to right as she stood there in the gloomy, blacked-out corridor, as if she half expected the police to raid the premises at any moment. "*Un petit cadeau pour vous, M'sieu.*" She smiled winningly.

"A present?" he echoed, puzzled.

"*Oui . . . une vierge,*" Madam said, as the girl lowered her gaze and looked at her wooden shoes, heeled with strips from an old bicycle.

Egan repeated the word, wondering what it meant. The Madam saw his bewilderment and looking at the girl's loins significantly, pursed her lips and pressed her blood-red fingers to them. "*Superbe!*" she exclaimed, as if assessing some fine gourmet dish. She gave the girl a gentle shove through the door, winked knowingly at Egan and then closed the door gently behind the newcomer, leaving the two young people to stare at each other in embarrassed bewilderment. But as puzzled as he was, Peter Egan knew what the Madam expected him to do with her 'present'.

All the same, although he felt a sense of exciting, rising lust, he didn't know how to start; he was too inexperienced and after all the peasant girl, if that was what she was, spoke no English. So it was that the girl herself took over and made it all very easy, even effortless for him, as he lay there on the bed, feeling a hot, tingling sensation between his legs and embarrassed and red-faced at what was happening down there – whether he liked it or not.

Not looking at her directly, he reached up and started undoing the buttons of her simple, cheap dress. She wasn't wearing a petticoat or a bra. Her heavy, firm breasts, with their large dun-coloured nipples, tumbled out and he stared at them, heart in his mouth. She didn't seem to notice, but continued with her unbuttoning until she was clad solely in a pair of shabby, pink rayon knickers and patched woollen stockings held up by twisted elastic garters. It was the simple costume of a poor working girl but in years to come, when he had enjoyed the services and pleasures of much more sophisticated and richer women,

178

whose underclothes were made of the finest silks, he had always recalled the wordless peasant girl standing there waiting for his command as the most exciting and exotic thing which had ever happened to him.

Finally she asked huskily as the brothel started to settle down with the noises becoming ever more muted: "*Maintenant?*"

"*Oui,*" he replied, hardly able to get the word out.

Wordlessly she got in beside him and he felt the sudden surge of healthy sexual warmth like that of some willing animal. She placed her rough and calloused hand on his erection. He sighed and blindly he groped for her sex. It was wet and warm. He touched her more firmly. It was her turn to sigh.

A minute later they were entwined together, bodies suddenly sweaty, their breath coming in hectic, delighted gasps, as the room rocked and outside, unknown to them who no longer cared (for there was only one world for them, one of passion and blind love) the real world fell apart.

He awoke to find her bending over him, her breasts nuzzling his flushed, but relaxed face, stroking his head gently and looking down at him tenderly, as a fond mother might do with a beloved child. "*Pauvre garçon,*" she whispered with sudden sadness, as if she knew already she would never see him again. "*Pauvre garçon . . .*"

Chapter Five

Sergeant Hands was a happy man. He looked fresh and alert, as if he had slept around the clock, when in fact he had had 30 minutes sleep at the most. The old Madam, creaky as her old bones were, had been very demanding – and highly pleasurable. More than once he had slapped her ample naked bottom as she had staggered out of the high brass bed to urinate in the enamel chamber pot underneath it. Once, with a gasp of awe after she had performed a trick on him that even he, with his vast sexual experience, had never come across, he had muttered, "God stone the ferkin' crows, you ain't half bad, you old cow!"

Now he was washed, his uniform brushed free of dirt, his face shaven and looking fuller as if he might well have just eaten a big meal.

Egan blinked in wonder as he stared up at the sergeant from the rumpled bed – the peasant girl had departed as silently as she had come – and breathed in wonder, after Sergeant Hands had announced, "It's the friggin' witching hour, sir. I've already stood 'em to."

Egan muttered, "You've even had a shave, Sergeant!" He rubbed his own unshaven face and added, "How did you do that? I lost my small pack with my shaving gear ages ago."

Sergeant Hands smiled, pleased that the young officer had noticed. "Got to blind the troops with bullshit, sir, if you'll forgive my French. Set a good example." He put his hand delicately in front of his mouth and coughed in an affected manner, as if he wished to hide his teeth. "I borrowed Madam's razor. Hence the nicks," he indicated the red marks covered by face powder at the side of his neck.

Peter laughed. "*Her razor?* Does she use it to shave her moustache?"

For the first time since Peter had known the little wizened old sweat, the latter looked embarrassed. "Not exactly her moustache, sir," he said hesitantly. "T'other end."

"The other end?" Peter queried, puzzled.

"Yessir! You see, sir, some of her – er – customers like a shaven beaver so she uses the little razor—"

"Holy cow!" Peter Egan broke in. "You mean you shaved yourself with the razor she uses to shave off her pubic hairs!" A huge grin spread across his face and he commented, "I think I'll keep my beard, thank you, Sarge!"

"Yes, sir," Hands agreed, "It is a bit o' a turnup for the book. I don't think I'll mention it in the sergeants' mess when we get back." He corrected himself, "*If* we get back!" Then he was brisk and businesslike once more, as Peter buckled on his battered equipment, Madam's 'beaver' forgotten. "It's slowly getting light outside."

"The Jerries?"

"Madam's been outside. She wanted to get some early morning grub, bread mainly – naturally she doesn't have to use coupons – for us. She sez there's no sign of the Jerries in this area."

181

Peter Egan nodded his thanks. "Excellent. All right. Are the wounded OK?"

"They are, sir, thank God. I don't know what we would have done if we'd had serious casualties. We'd have bin right in the shit."

"Feed 'em then," Peter Egan continued urgently, realising for the first time the dangers the new day might bring.

"Yessir. And what do we do when we clear the Old Port?"

Peter Egan looked annoyed, as if it were a question that he had been refusing to answer all along. "We'll worry about that when we get that far, Sarge. All right get on with it."

"Sir," Hands clicked to attention and got on with it, telling himself as he went out at the double that the young Canadian officer was learning fast; there was no denying the authority in his voice now.

They were 40 or 50 officers from the *Wehrmacht* or *Kriegsmarine*, the kind that the ordinary German soldier or sailor called contemptous 'base stallions': men who hoped to sit the war out behind an office desk, never to hear a shot fired in anger. They would die in bed of old age.

Now, in their elegant uniforms, hanging on to their ornate swords and dirks importantly, they postured and exclaimed for the benefit of the 'Poisoned Dwarf's'* cameramen and reporters who were everywhere on the

---

* Dr Joseph Goebbels, German Minister of Propaganda, known thus on account of his small size and vitriolic tongue.

deck of the battle-shattered *Campbeltown*. Watching them play their little games, there were perhaps another 350 German sailors and soldiers standing on the debris-littered quayside. They spent the time pleasurably, smoking their cigarettes in a leisurely fashion, wondering why the Tommies had gone to such efforts to beach the antiquated destroyer the way they had.

Thus they chatted and postured, their stomachs rumbling noisely, for in the German Armed Forces breakfast consisted of a cup of weak acorn coffee and a thin slice of black bread smeared with ersatz jam, made of turnips and rosehips. But their thoughts were of the evening in the Old Port where their worthless marks would buy them whores and not gut booze.

Not that the elegant officers parading along the crumpled deck, with the inert shapes of the dead still lying there under blood-stained blankets, worried about such lowly matters. They had their French mistresses, with their dyed black hair and expensive Parisian dresses, who knew how to make a man happy with their naughty if delightful '*Amour à la francais*'. Everyone knew just how decadent the French women were. As they always maintained – without too much conviction – "No decent German woman would do things like that. The Führer wouldn't tolerate it!"

Then it happened – suddenly, surprisingly, shockingly!

A low roar. A trembling of the steel deck. Thin wisps of grey smoke erupting between every loose plate. They looked at each other in alarm. The roar grew in volume and the old destroyer started to tremble violently. *What in three devils' names was going on, Gottverdamme?*

Now all thoughts of good French red wine, decadent piggery in French whores' bedrooms, binges in the Old Port, vanished as that terrible roaring fury drowned all

183

other sound, all other thoughts fleeing save that of one terrible overwhelming fear of death. It smashed forth from below the wildly bucking deck beneath their feet, spilling scarlet flame over their bodies, filling the air with thick choking cordite fumes, hurling the German officers and men high into the morning air, sweeping the terrified other ranks from the quayside to vanish in the terrifying great blowtorch of flame which swept the deck, consuming their flesh, turning them into grotesque, charred pygmies.

Exactly on time, the five tons of high explosive hidden in the bows of the *Campbeltown* had detonated, catching the victorious Germans totally by surprise. Now as the French and German ambulances, sirens shrieking their urgent message of doom, raced to the disaster, those who had survived panicked. They fled screaming and jostling each other in their unreasoning haste, trampling over the bodies of the dying and broken-limbed bodies lying everywhere, discipline and restraint thrown to the winds.

Now the German victors, who five minutes before were supremely confident in their recent triumph over the Tommies, lost all control. Their panic was increased even more by the delayed charges which started to explode all over the Old Port and *Forme Écluse*. In their defeat the commandos were now taking their revenge. Everywhere explosions, large and small, wrecked the dawn stillness.

"They're attacking again!" the soldiers cried in sudden alarm. "Shoot the swine down, and the treacherous French. They've been hiding them all the time, the rotten swine!"

The Germans began firing indiscriminately at the French workers, cigarettes glued to their bottom lips, as they wheeled their shabby old cycles into the dockyard

184

to commence the day's work. Machine-gun fire raked the windows of the many waterside bars and cafes catering for their early morning needs. Somebody threw a grenade at one of the trams jingling its way into the confusion. It bucked like a wild horse, scattering dead and dying workers from the platform onto the suddenly blood-stained *pavé*.

"Cease firing!" officers yelled, red-faced and fuming. "Stop that, you stupid bastards!" the chaindogs cried, smashing into the panicking troops with the brass-shod butts of their carbines. "It's all over, you arses-with-ears!" NCOs cursed. But the soldiers took no notice. In their unreasoning fear, they continued to shoot at anything and everything which didn't wear the field-grey of the *Wehrmacht*.

Now it was the turn of the French dock workers to panic. They broke ranks and fled back from the docks over the single surviving bridge from the *Forme Écluse* to the *Bassin Penhouet* leaving their dead and dying everywhere on the bloody cobbles. A troop of German civilian workers in the uniform of the *Todt* Organisation tried to stop then. To no avail. The French simply swept them to one side.

And now the handful of French Resistance in the great port started to take a hand in the game, sniping at the *boche* from upstairs windows, dropping home-made bombs upon their heads, setting fire to their vehicles with Molotov cocktails and, in the midst of all that confusion, knowing that, temporarily at least, they were safe from the German wireless detection and listening service which usually patrolled the street of St Nazaire on the alert for illegal broadcasts, and the secret radio operators began to contact their masters in London . . .

185

In the British capital, the messages from the other side of the Channel had been picked up and decoded within the hour. One hour after that they were in the hands of Mountbatten himself. For the latter was keeping a close watch on the operation. He was desperate for further promotion, and, naturally, a new 'gong'. Thus it was that he guarded all information coming from France, feeding an impatient Churchill with that news only which he felt it was suitable for the Prime Minister to hear.

"You need not tell me, Mountbatten," the PM exclaimed joyfully as soon as the Head of Combined Operations entered his office, his eyes shining. "*It worked!*"

"Like a charm!" Mountbatten lied. "We've just learned from our agents in France that they've rammed the lock gate and shortly thereafter all five tons of HE in the *Campbeltown* went up, taking a large number of Germans with it."

"Bravo, Dickie!" Churchill clapped his pudgy hands together like a small child learning that he had just been promised an expensive toy. "That puts paid to the *Tirpitz's* venture into the North Atlantic, I should think." Suddenly he dabbed his wet eyes with a large silk handkerchief, as if the emotion were too much for him.

"How many casualties?" he asked a moment later, pulling himself together.

"The Navy got back with only fairly slight casualties," Mountbatten answered. He frowned suddenly and stopped speaking.

"And the Army?" Churchill prompted.

"Well, PM, we know that they suffered severe casualties in the first assault. But a lot of Colonel Newman's people got ashore and obviously from what we've just heard about the delayed charges there must have been enough of them to carry out their assigned tasks—" He ceased speaking again.

"But you don't know what happened to them then, Dickie?" Churchill said gently, the usual defiant growl absent from his voice.

"No, sir."

"So we're missing most of Two Commando?"

"Yessir. But we haven't given them up for good, sir," Mountbatten added, hastily remembering that 'gong'.

Churchill didn't seem to hear. As outside the sombre chimes of Big Ben sounded, booming away their lives with metallic inexorability, he considered. Finally he broke the heavy, brooding silence of his office with: "Dickie, you must go over to max effort. We owe everything to those commando chaps wherever they are and whatever shape they are in, they must be brought back. Is that understood?" He looked fiercely at the handsome young naval commander.

"Of course, sir," Mountbatten answered with more enthusiasm than he felt. "You can rely on me and my chaps." Minutes later he was walking slowly and thoughtfully down the great, echoing marble steps, his mind full, telling himself that the surviving commandos didn't have a hope in hell now the balloon had gone up. He frowned and almost forgot to return the marine sentry's salute. "Balls!" he said to himself, "I've had that gong . . . !" And with that he had vanished into the wartime traffic of the capital.

Chapter Six

Peter Egan crouched behind the wall, listening to the cries of rage and confusion. Next to him Sergeant Hands and the rest crouched impatiently. They didn't need the young Canadian officer to tell them that this was their only chance of escaping while the confusion was at its height. Unfortunately a dozen or so German sailors had gone to ground to their immediate front. Once the escapers rose, the Germans couldn't help but see them at once. Peter wondered what their reaction would be, but he told himself they'd fire a few shots at least before they did a bunk – if they did a bunk.

"Well, sir?" Hands asked.

Peter Egan knew there was no use postponing a decision any longer. "Well, Sarge, it's either piss or get off the pot," Even as he said the words, he was surprised at his newly found crudeness. He supposed it came with the brutalisation of combat.

"Agreed, sir."

Egan tapped the sole remaining magazine of his tommygun. "Prepare to move out, lads," he said, more confidence in his voice than he really felt. *"LET'S GO!"*

The surviving commandos needed no urging. They knew, even the most stupid of them, that this was their last chance of escape. Sergeant Hands grunted and flung his last remaining grenade to his front. As it clattered and rolled along the cobbles the suddenly alerted German sailors yelled in alarm "*'Tommies – die greifen an!'*"

In the instant that Hands's grenade burst into a bright, angry scarlet light, ragged fire opened up from the German positions. Here and there a commando skidded to an abrupt halt and went down cursing and groaning. But the rest kept on. Hands snarled and, using his entrenching tool like an axe, sliced the head of a young seaman in half. His brain matter oozed out of the gaping wound in his skull, the bone glistening like polished ivory. Everywhere the commandos had closed with the German sailors in their floppy blue caps with the flowing ribbons. Grunting and cursing they hacked, gouged, thrust, chopped, with no quarter given or taken. When a man went down he was trampled and kicked to death by the gasping, crazed victor. Peter had no time to think then, but later he realised he had been party not to a minor battle skirmish, but to a hot-blooded massacre.

Then they were through, with the surviving Germans running and throwing away their weapons in their fear, as if pursued by the hounds of hell themselves.

Panting and lathered in sweat, slinging over their shoulder those of their wounded comrades who could no longer walk, the survivors staggered on, eyes wide and wild like men demented. Soon the alarm would be sounded once more, and again every man's hand would be against them. They *had* to get out of St Nazaire soon, or they would never get out.

A deadly game of cat and mouse began as they wound in and out of the narrow alleys of the Old Port, with the old houses on both sides tightly shuttered and silent, as if long abandoned. But the fugitives knew instinctively that that wasn't the case. Behind those barred windows the civilians crouched fearfully, tensed for the first sign of trouble.

Twice they dodged patrols of German soldiers searching for them in that confused area, springing over garden walls with new-found energy, fear pumping adrenaline into their weary bodies, doubling frantically down back alleys with angry tracer stitching a pattern of death at their flying heels. They crashed through locked doors in their frantic haste. Once Egan went flying through into a *salon* and found a woman holding her plump legs high in the air while a skinny runt of a Frenchman, his yellow rump naked, pumped away at her loins as if his very life depended upon it. He even had no time to laugh.

They found a wood-burning German truck and fumbled with the unfamiliar controls, but all they succeeded in doing was to sound the horn in a long, shrill blast which attracted fresh fire their way once more. They abandoned the vehicle and ran on, blundering and floundering in the backstreet maze, trying desperately to find a way out.

They found themselves outside what looked like a ship's painter's warehouse. There were rows of neatly stacked paint drums everywhere. The pursuit had died down, but they could proceed no farther. There was a sniper concealed somewhere in the warehouse. Every time one of them moved, he fired, and because he was using smokeless powder in his rounds it was difficult to pinpoint him.

"Fuck this for a game of soldiers," Sergeant Hands swore in exasperation. "Look at that boat over there," pointing to the large motorboat anchored in the channel a mere 50 feet or so beyond the warehouse. But it might have been 500 miles way with that sniper barring their progress. Hands's temper carried him away. "Roll on death and let's have a fuck at the angels!" he yelled and before Egan could stop him he was charging forward, tommy-gun chattering furiously at his waist. Suddenly he skidded to a halt. For one heart-stopping moment, Egan thought he had been hit. But the little old sweat was merely changing the gun's magazine.

Now, like some Western gunslinger in a Hollywood movie, he stood there at the half-crouch, legs spread apart, spraying the warehouse and the paint cans with the full magazine.

For one long second nothing happened. Suddenly there was a great frightening hush, then the front of the warehouse burst into a fierce flame. The cans popped and exploded. The fire crept across the cobbles, turning them a dull purple. The air seared the watchers' faces, and sucked the very air from their lungs so that they found themselves gasping and choking like asthmatics in the moment of a fatal attack. Opposite the halted commandos, the sniper writhed frantically on the burning cobbles, his hands, with which he tried to beat out the fire creeping ever higher up to his poor body, already alight.

But at that moment the commandos were too desperate to feel any pity for the dying man, his charred body visibly shrinking before their eyes in that terrible heat. "At the double, lads," Egan cried above the crackle of flames, "Follow me – *quick!*"

They needed no urging. All of them knew that their luck wouldn't hold out much longer. As they ran past the dying sniper someone emptied a magazine into his tortured, contorted body and his writhing stopped. As they ran on, he lay still, blue flames eating his charred skull almost leisurely. "Save yer friggin' ammo," Sergeant

191

Hands grunted and then they were clambering down the green-slicked quay wall towards the launch, their last hope of salvation.

On the craft, Egan looked a little puzzled at the many controls. He had sailed boats back on the Lakes in Canada as a boy, including motorboats, but he had never been confronted with the complicated controls of a high-speed naval craft.

The others looked at him anxiously and again he felt that sense of responsibility for their lives. "Do you think you can manage her, sir?" Sergeant Hands broke the tense silence. "I know how to steer one of them commando landing barges, but that's about it."

Egan forced a laugh, but at that moment he had never felt less like laughing. "Well, now's the time to find out," he said and turned the main switch. The instrument panel lit up immediately, green and red needles swinging into position. He glanced hastily along the panel. "*Essence*, that means petrol, I guess," he said, as if he were speaking to himself, then raising his voice. "Well, the tank seems half full, that should be enough to get us back to Eng – old Blighty." He used the old soldier's word in order to make the tense survivors feel more at ease.

While they waited apprehensively, he ran his fingers carefully over the controls, pushing them or pulling them out as he felt fit. Suddenly, the motor-launch's engines erupted into violent, noisy activity. The whole craft seemed to shake, as if some tremendous, harnessed power was impatient to be released. "Cast off!" he yelled above the racket to the commando at the stern.

Hastily the commando, who could use only one hand – his other was bloody and bandaged – undid the wet knot. "Ready to go, sir!" he yelled in decidedly unnautical language.

Hands, the stickler for the correct drill under all circumstances, even ones such as this, with death lurking behind every corner, shook his head in disapproval.

Gingerly, Egan eased the throttle forward, saying a silent prayer that he would get it right and not stall the engines, for at the back of his mind he could already hear the sounds of German military vehicles approaching. He didn't need a crystal ball to know that the Germans were on their way to the docks. Jerkily the motorboat began to move into the channel. White water surged up at her sharply cut bow. "You're doing it right, sir," Hands gushed.

"Yes, like the actress said to the bishop," Egan grinned.

Hands didn't laugh; he was too tense. Behind them the howl of hurrying motors grew ever louder. "Some of you who ain't wounded," Hands shouted, "On the deck, and get ready for the bastards!"

"Prepare to repel boarders, eh, Sarge!" a slightly hysterical voice called back.

"Yer'll have my friggin' ammo boot up yer skinny arse, if you don't move it smartish!" Hands threatened.

The commando duly moved 'smartish'.

Sweat beaded Egan's furrowed brow in spite of the early morning coolness and the stiff breeze coming off the sea. He treated the controls with kid gloves. Too much power, he knew, and the big engines would land the boat in the mudflats on the opposite bank. Too little and she might stall, leaving her at mid-stream and at the mercy of the Germans who were already piling out of their vehicles, cursing and unslinging their weapons as they doubled to the edge of the jetty. There was some desultory fire from the commandos still on deck, but it was weak; for Sergeant Hands had cautioned the survivors, "Keep five rounds in reserve. Yer don't know what the Jerries might do. Their dander's friggin' well up after that explosion on the *Campbeltown!*"

"Ay, sarge," a corporal had agreed. "Yer don't need to draw us no friggin' picture. We all know what they'll do to us *now!*"

Peter Egan frowned when he heard the statement. The man might well be right. In their unreasoning rage the Germans might well just stand them up against the nearest wall and 'liquidate' them, as they called it. Now, those grim words lent even more urgency to his efforts, as the first slugs started to patter against the sides of the slowly moving launch, chipping out slivers of wood and whining off the metal superstructure. If he didn't get away soon, the whole waterfront would be alive with enemy fire. Carefully, he opened the throttle a little wider. The launch's sharp prow rose out of the water. At the stern, a white wake appeared. Beneath his feet he could feel the craft begin to shake like a live thing as the engines took hold. Hastily he said a silent prayer that he was doing it right.

"That's the stuff, sir!" Sergeant Hands began. Next moment he cursed and clapped a horny hand to his right shoulder, the blood already spurting out in a scarlet arc. "Fuck it!" he cursed through teeth gritted with pain, "the sods have gorn and shot me!"

"Hang on, Sarge!" a commando cried above the hectic racket, "I'll get my field dressing."

"No yer won't," Hands snarled, supporting himself against the bridge, his face very pale and contorted with pain. "Watch yer friggin' front, man!"

Peter Egan knew he had to take one last desperate chance. If he didn't, the rest would follow Sergeant Hands; at that range the Jerries couldn't miss. "Hit the deck everyone!" he yelled and, not waiting to check whether his handful of survivors had obeyed the order, he pushed the throttle wide open.

The motor launch responded immediately. With a powerful jerk that nearly threw him to the deck, it surged forward. Suddenly a great bone of whirling white water appeared to his front. He narrowed his eyes and tried to peer through it, although it was almost blinding him. He prayed that the channel went straight ahead.

Behind, the infuriated Germans grew smaller and smaller. Then others, farther up the channel took up the challenge. Scarlet flame stabbed the grey gloom on both sides of the racing launch. There was the hollow boom of a bigger weapon. A white blur hurtled towards the escaping launch. "Christ All-Friggin'-Mighty!" Hands cursed. "They're using frigging AP* now!"

They ducked instinctively as the shell shrieked above their heads. It disappeared into the distance and someone cried with relief. "Hell's bells, I nearly pissed mesen then!"

"*Nearly!* I fuckin' well did!" someone else said mournfully.

Under other circumstances, Peter Egan would have laughed at that typical coarse English humour, which had carried these soldiers through many a hard time, but not now. Everything was too touch-and-go. One false move and that would be that.

Up front, where the channel entered the River Loire,

* Armour-piercing ammunition.

red and white flares were rising into the grey sky to fall slowly, colouring everything in their unreal sickly hue. Egan knew instinctively that it was a signal to naval craft farther up the great river. For all he knew they were starting up their engines already, preparing to move out and stop the fleeing launch before she reached the sea.

His heart sank. After all they had been through, they were going to be pipped at the post, as the dead Howling Mad had often phrased. Then farther ahead, perhaps half a mile or so away, he saw something else which filled his weary body with new hope.

His red-rimmed eyes peered down the Loire, as he willed the launch to make it. Then he yelled *"FOG!"* in a hoarse voice, sounding like some parched traveller in a trackless desert. "Up ahead – there's *FRIGGING FOG* . . . !"

Chapter Seven

They seemed to be the last men alive in the world. A thick, freezing, unseasonal fog had engulfed the stolen launch as Egan, still at the wheel, though his eyes felt as if someone had thrown sand in them, steered her in the general direction of England.

The unwounded commandos had found some hard German salami, even harder black bread with what looked like ends of straw sticking out of the loaves, plus – most welcome of all – a small crate of Munich beer. Under an ashen-faced Hands's supervision the food and beer had been rationed and passed out first to more seriously wounded; the rest had followed.

Now, with the commandos divided into two watches, a commando who had been an East End tailor in civilian life was sewing up canvas shrouds for those who had died since they had boarded the launch. Egan had watched him for a while, as the man had squatted cross-legged on the deck, singing a little Yiddish ditty, but when the ex-tailor had thrust the curved sailmaker's needle through the dead man's nose before finishing sewing up the rest of the shroud, he had turned, sickened, and walked away quickly. Later Hands had enlightened him that it had been the traditional 'last stitch', which dated back to Nelson's times. The old hands still used it to ascertain if the 'dead' man was really dead. That one had been, as had the rest.

Egan had now forgotten the dead, telling himself the living were more important. As tired as he was, his primary duty was to get them back safely to an English port; and it looked as if he were going to be able to do it. The fog was providing excellent cover and although he had slowed the engines down twice and ordered the deck watch to listen intently for any other sound in that thick, grey mist, there had been nothing. The fog was obviously hampering the German chase, too. Perhaps they had given up, he told himself hopefully, now that they had beaten the English off and were concentrating on getting St Nazaire patched up and in working order as soon as possible. After all, the port was also vital to their U-boat wolf packs roaming the Allied convoy routes.

Half an hour later the motor-launch commenced taking water. At first it was hardly perceptible. At the controls, Egan, who had just taken over from Hands, who was attempting to steer the best he could in spite of his wound, noticed that the German craft seemed a little sluggish. He thought that it ought to be doing better now that her displacement was being lightened as she used more and more fuel. Otherwise he thought nothing more of it, concentrating on steering his way through the rolling fogbanks.

Some time after that, however, he received urgent word from below where the more seriously wounded were packed side by side on the deck, that sea water was beginning to seep in and soak their blood-stained uniforms. Hastily Egan had them moved to the upper deck and covered with blankets they had found, then went to have a look himself. They were right. Already the lower deck was knee-deep in icy sea water and more was pouring in all the time. He reduced the speed of the launch, reasoning that the craft had been hit in the hull during the escape to the Loire. Obviously the hole was beneath the waterline and as he stood there a little helplessly, feeling the vessel becoming more sluggish and unwieldly by the minute, he puzzled about what he could do. One thing was certain: the German motor-launch would never reach the English coast, while taking water at the rate that she was at the moment.

It was Sergeant Hands, looking very white, with his face twisted as if he were in some pain, who made his decision – indirectly – for him. "Sir, there's no other way. We'll have to heave to and see if we can't patch up the hole down there. Otherwise we'll—" he didn't need to finish the rest of his sentence. Egan knew what he meant – *they'd sink*. "Agreed," he said reluctantly.

With England miles away and the possibility that the fog might clear, leaving them wide open for marauding German planes, he hated to waste any further time. "But what about pumps? We'll have to clear the lower hold of water if we're going to get at the hole." He threw a look over the side. Thick blue-grey oil was leaking from somewhere. Somehow it looked obscene to his unpractised eye, like pus seeping from a badly septic wound. But of the wound – the hole which was causing their current problem – there was no sign.

"Don't look too rosy, sir," Hands said softly, following the direction of his gaze. "But we *have* got pumps for starters, sir."

Five minutes later, Sergeant Hands had assembled the commandos, including the lightly wounded, who he thought capable of working. Egan wasted no time as he addressed them, the wet fog whirling about him so that at times he looked like a grey spectre; with the drops of water dripping mournfully from the brim of his battered cap. "All right, lads," he said urgently, "I'll make it snappy. You're not gonna like this – it's going to be hard work – but it has to be done."

Hands glared around their drawn, weary faces, as if challenging them to make a comment. No one did.

"We'll try to get rid of all unnecessary weight. First the anchor and the steel anchor cable. They're both bloody heavy. Then anything else, except the twin machine-guns. You never know," he hinted darkly, but didn't go any further into the matter. "Once we've lightened her we'll heave to, see if we can patch up the hole beneath the waterline, and get on our way again. But remember," he raised a dirty finger in warning. "time's running out!"

"Ay, that it is," Hands added, "so just don't stand there like spare cocks at a wedding. Get yer friggin' fingers out and get started . . . !"

All of them knew that the old sweat was right, but before they moved off to carry out Egan's instructions one of them cried, "Three cheers for the OC, lads!"

Egan looked at them as they raised their hands, wondering if he could believe the evidence of his own eyes. He had got them into this mess and now it was doubtful if they would survive to reach their home country, but here they were cheering *him!*

As the first "Hip-hip" rang out lustily, he turned away quickly so that they wouldn't see the sudden tears in his red-rimmed eyes.

*　　*　　*

While the survivors laboured, fighting a race with death, back in England wartime life went on as normal. After all, it was Saturday. As men returned flushed and happy from their local football matches, the women crimped and curled their hair in readiness for the Saturday night out at the pubs, the *Palais de danse*, the 'flicks'. The kids clamoured for their sweet coupons and the old folks in their slippers prepared for their Saturday-night treat from the fish shop, with lashings of HP sauce if they were lucky.

But while the man in the street relaxed, flush with the good wages that everyone was earning in the munitions factories these days, a handful of men still concentrated on the fighting and the fates of obscure men like Egan and his commandos, battling for their lives in the Channel.

At his country retreat, Churchill was taking the latest message on the great raid from Mountbatten in London. The latter filled the Prime Minister in about weather, casualties and what little was known of the survivors of the 2nd Commando, while Churchill dipped the end of his glowing cigar in the glass of fine pre-war French cognac and listened attentively.

Mountbatten was just explaining that the Channel was fogged in and making it difficult for Coastal Command to spot any survivors of Colonel Newman's ill-fated force, when the PM growled, "But the weather has been excellent here. Sunshine most of the afternoon, Dickie. No problems there for the Sunderlands of Coastal Command."

The Head of Combined Operations didn't react so Churchill, growing impatient with what he thought was Mountbatten's lack of initiative, growled, "What of the German wireless service, Dickie? Have they made any reports about our chaps trying to make a break for it by sea, eh?"

Mountbatten seemed to hesitate, or so it seemed to Churchill. Finally he replied, "Well, PM, one of our listening stations at Dover picked up a garbled Hun message."

Churchill grinned at Mountbatten's use of the word 'Hun'. Wasn't he a 100 per cent 'Hun' himself? After all, his father had changed his name from the German 'Battenberg' to 'Mountbatten' due to pressure from the anti-German lobby back at the turn of the century. "And?" he demanded.

"Well, as I say, PM, it was garbled. But as far as the experts can tell, it states that a group of our commando chaps escaped in a stolen German launch and an air search has been ordered to find them."

"So there you are, Dickie. If the *Huns*," he emphasized the word maliciously, "can fly, so can Coastal Command."

"But, sir," Mountbatten objected. "Those Sunderlands are very precious to Coastal Command. They can't afford to lose them."

"*Commodore*," Churchill said harshly, "So are my soldiers, and we can't afford to lose them either, especially as they are risking their lives like this."

"But, sir, even if they did take off how could the Sunderlands find a small boat in the middle of the Channel in a damned peasouper?"

"There are no buts!" Churchill snapped angrily, "and those honest, humble soldiers are precious, too." His indignation was all too obvious and, back in London, Mountbatten realised immediately just how serious the PM was. He wouldn't hesitate to sack a commander, even if he was King George's cousin. "I agree, sir," he said hastily. "I'll get on to Coastal Command immediately."

"Do that," Churchill answered silkily. He put down the phone, puffed on the cigar and followed it by a sip of the fine old brandy. Ever since the Mountbattens had arrived in England back in Queen Victoria's time, straight from Germany, they had been on the make. It was very opportune that they should be taken down a peg or two every now and again. Besides his commandos *were* more precious than a four-engined flying boat. He knew now that Mountbatten would do his utmost to rescue those men in the stolen German motorboat. He chuckled to himself. If Mountbatten didn't, he would find the King-Emperor, cousin that he was, would *not* be awarding a precious 'gong' to a man who desired them like a miser craved for gold . . .

They had worked their guts out all that long Saturday afternoon, pumping the hold dry in an attempt to find the hole beneath the waterline while two of the more seriously wounded lay in their blood-stained blankets on the wet deck, acting as lookouts whenever they regained consciousness before lapsing into a pain-racked blackness once more.

The dumping of the ton-weight anchor and anchor chain had been the most difficult task for the virtually exhausted men. They had been forced to haul them out of the locker by hand, link by link, the men's faces greasy with sweat, their muscles red-hot and on fire, threatening to burst under the tremendous strain at every fresh effort.

They couldn't find a pump to bale the water out of the lower deck, so that had been done laboriously by hand, too, with a chain of men, some wounded, staggering visibly as they passed one heavy bucket after another to the man above them. Time had passed leadenly in back-breaking labour with the men gasping and wheezing, ready, or so it appeared, to drop at any moment.

But they hadn't. By 1500, with the fog obviously thinning out as they hit the warm front coming from the west, they had cleared away the heavy weights and drained the lower deck to ankle-depth.

Now Egan ordered a break. The beer had all gone, but Sergeant Hands, with his old soldier's nose for finding things – often before they had been lost – had discovered two bottles of schnapps, "Real paint-stripper stuff, they tell me, sir!", he had reported delightedly to Egan. "But it'll put a bit o' lead into their pencils, I'll be bound!" Now, Egan issued two teaspoonfuls of the firewater, which made the men choke, gasp and turn scarlet. All the same, the German *Korn* had the desired effect. For a while, Egan knew, it would put new life into them and he fully recognised that they needed it if they were going to make their escape before the German *Luftwaffe* turned up. For the fog was clearing ever more rapidly and he guessed the Germans would soon have planes out looking for survivors of the raid.

Within five minutes of 'splicing the mainbrace', as Hands had called the spirit ration in an affected manner which he supposed was used by naval officers, they had found the jagged hole in the hull. Immediately, they started patching it up with whatever came to hand; mattresses, bunk 'biscuits', several pieces of old sailcloth, any blankets that could be spared from the seriously wounded. As one of the weary commandos complained without rancour, "If this friggin' well goes on, they'll have the pants off'n me, I swear!" To which Hands had remarked. "And that'd be a splendid sight, young

Jones!" He licked his lips melodramatically and curled an imaginary moustache, "Now where's my Vaseline?"

Half hour later the job had been finished. The water had almost ceased coming through the jagged gap in the hull, save for a trickle here and there. Egan stood poised at the wheel. A commando waited at the head of the companionway leading below. Down below, Sergeant Hands was watching the gap. At the first sign of trouble he would signal to the commando and the man would pass the word on to a tense Egan.

"All right, stand tight! Here we go," Egan called and pressed the starter button. The powerful engines sprang into noisy life at once. The hull quivered. The engines rumbled, ready to be let off the leash like highly trained dogs.

Gingerly, very gingerly, Egan eased the throttle forward. His eyes were glued almost hypnotically to the rev indicator. The red needle flickered, then with the slightest of jerks the launch started to move across the sea through an area almost clear of fog.

Tensely Egan waited for the first cry from the commando stationed at the top of the companionway. Nothing came. He gave the battered craft a little more power. She was now moving at perhaps five knots. He threw a glance over the bow. Nothing! Then he could contain his anxiety no longer. Without taking his gaze off the control panel for one moment, and ready to cut the engine in a flash he called, "How's it looking down there, soldier?"

There was a pause as the soldier passed the query down below to the sergeant watching the patched up hole. Then came: "Right as rain, sir. Ain't taking no water to speak of, sir!"

Egan ignored the terrible grammar. He didn't even

notice it. He called back, "Keep an eye on it, soldier – and *thanks*." Then he concentrated on gingerly forcing another couple of knots out of the German boat, for the fog had about vanished now and he didn't need a crystal ball to realise that the German Air Force would be soon stooging around, looking for targets among the survivors of the great raid on St Nazaire.

The weary Canadian was not far wrong. As the first brown smudge on the afternoon horizon indicated that they were approaching England at last and Egan was already indulging himself in fantasies of hot baths, bacon and eggs (*two*, a rare treat in egg-rationed England), and perhaps a small whisky afterwards, a lookout's voice rang out with "Aircraft off the port bow," and then in a tone which Egan would categorise later as 'a damned bloody moan' – "*JERRIES!*"

Chapter Eight

Oberleutnant Hartung was in a bad mood. He had one hell of a headache from too much bubbly the previous night, when the *Geschwader* had celebrated the great victory at St Nazaire; and he was angry, very angry. He had been snoring and fast asleep in a happy state of oblivion in the duty room when the orderly officer had woken him roughly to tell him he was to take the early morning Heinkel out; the Tommies had been spotted. A U-boat permanently stationed off the English coast on the lookout for Tommy coastal convoys had seen the battered, stolen launch, packed with the Tommies from St Nazaire.

He had licked his cracked, parched lips and had felt the first unpleasant movements down in his pubic area which heralded crabs, as he knew from long experience, before he had asked grumpily, "Why me, *Leutnant*? Why didn't the blue boys put a tin fish up her arse there and then and have done with the buck-toothed Tommies, eh?"

"*Es tut mir leid, Herr Oberleutnant*," the young duty officer had apologised, "but Naval High Command says it can't afford to waste an expensive torpedo on the craft in question."

Despite his raging headache and the crabs, he had cursed for five minutes without using the same word twice. That had been six hours ago. Now he had been droning up and down the Channel for what seemed an eternity trying to penetrate the fog and spot the enemy craft, his anger growing by the instant. Now, finally, the nose turret gunner sang out the bearing and added joyfully, as if he were having a great time, "It's them all right, *Oberleutnant* – and they haven't spotted us yet!"

Hartung muttered something and, taking care that no one was watching, he pulled out his silver flask and took a hefty swig of the cognac in it. It was German rotgut – cheap *Weinbrandverschnitt* – but he knew it would settle his stomach, which always seemed to do backflips whenever he was about to go into action.

Now, with new energy coursing through his blood, the crabs forgotten for the moment, *Oberleutnant* Hartung thrust the stick forward, saying through his throat mike, "*ATTACK . . . ATTACK . . . ATTACK!*"

Carried away by the excitement of the kill and it promised to be an easy one, for the Tommies below had still not spotted them, the air crew tensed behind their weapons, as lying flat on the deck of the sleek Heinkel bomber, the bomb-aimer peered through his sight, ready to drop his deadly eggs and destroy the unsuspecting Tommies.

They came lower and lower. Angry as he was, Hartung was still careful. He had seen too many of his fellow pilots 'buy the farm' because they had been careless when attacking what appeared to be an easy target. The battered motor-launch grew bigger and bigger by the instant. He could see the wires and bits of the radio aerial trailing over the side and the fresh, shiny gouges in its metal super-structure where it had been hit in the fight at St Nazaire; and as yet the tiny figures below had still not reacted.

He came down lower, skimming above the surface. His props churned the water into a white, frothy frenzy. It was dangerous flying that low, Hartung knew that. But at wave-top height he presented the smallest and most difficult target once the gunners on the launch below started to react.

"Tally ho, skipper!" the bomb-aimer cried jubilantly over the intercom, "I'll take over now."

"*Einverstanden*," Hartung answered automatically. It was standard operational procedure in the *Luftwaffe*. Once they were above the target, the bomb-aimer ran the plane. The pilot, whatever his rank, was reduced to the level of a driver, carrying out the bomb-aimer's orders. After all, that was what a bomber was for: bomb and destroy a target.

They came ever lower, skimming the waves at six metres now, with the bomb-aimer's gentle, careful voice through the intercom at regular intervals as he guided the pilot into the last stages of his approach and attack. "Steady . . . steady . . . too fast . . . steady . . . *We're going in now, skipper* . . . !"

"Hit 'em, Corporal!" Hands urged, feeling weak and sick, as he stood behind the man tensed at the old-fashioned Lewis gun, holding the spare mag. "You won't have much time—" The words died on his lips as the Heinkel's nose-gunner fired a burst, the slugs thwacking into the water all around the slow motor-launch. It was the signal for the final attack!

The corporal didn't hesitate. He pulled the wooden butt of the World War One machine-gun into his right shoulder and pressed the trigger. The Lewis stuttered into frenetic action and a burst of white tracer streamed towards the blue-painted bomber. Hartung laughed scornfully. "Stick yer peashooter up your arse, Tommy!" he commented contemptuously. "That's not even gonna give me a friggin' headheache!" He hunched over the controls, ignoring the white tracer streaming past the cockpit, intent on the kill, everything else forgotten as he listened to the bomb-aimer's quiet calculated instructions.

Down below, praying that he didn't disturb the patch on the hull, Egan, sweat pouring down his face, eased the craft to port. He did so just in time. In that instant, the bomber thundered over, momentarily blocking out all the light, a dark, lethal shape dropping from its blue-painted belly.

The bomb hit the sea some 50 yards away. There was a tremendous explosion. Wild white water hurtled upwards in a crazy geyser. The little boat violently rocked back and forth. Its superstructure touched the water, or so it seemed. For one horrifying moment, Egan, his heart in his mouth, thought she would go under. But, battered as she was, the launch was tough, righting herself as the twin-engined bomber soared high into the sky to execute a tight turn, thin black smoke trailing suddenly from its hard-pressed engines.

At the Lewis gun, the corporal sagged. "Come on!" Hands snapped angrily, "Digit out the friggin' orifice, man! Reload! The sod's coming in for another—?" The words died on his lips. In the instant that he ordered the gunner to take the spare maguzine, the man sagged. Slowly, limply he slid to the deck, the gun still cradled in his arms, almost as if he were preparing to go to sleep.

Hands's mouth dropped open in shocked amazement. The whole of the corporal's front had been ripped open by a cruel shard of red-hot shrapnel from the bomb, and his guts were slittering out of the hole like a steaming, sinister

210

snake. "God save and bless us!" Hands said thickly and crossed himself for the first time since he had been kicked out of his church for playing with a little girl in Father O'Keefe's confessional.

But already the Heinkel had completed its turn. Now, once more, Hartung was coming in low, face set and angry behind his goggles, listening still to the calm voice of the bomb-aimer over the intercom, who did not seem put out because the first bomb had missed. Though, undoubtedly, Hartung told himself, when he got back he would tell his comrades in the Sergeants' Mess, "Pissed as always, the skipper was. He couldn't hit a barn door the way he hits the fire water. I thought to myself it's gonna be trouble if we missed her a second time."

"No, well *Oberleutnant* Hartung will *not* miss her a second time," the pilot said grimly to no one in particular. "Arse-with-ears, just get me onto the target and you'll friggin' well see!" Once more he dived, this time determined to finish off the escaping launch.

On the bridge, the only sounds being the steady, muted throb of the engines and in the distance the roar of the Heinkel coming in for the next attack, Egan braced himself for the inevitable. Instinctively he knew that their sole defence – the Lewis gun – was out of action. Here and there unwounded commandos were poised, rifles upraised, ready to tackle the approaching bomber. But Egan knew they didn't have a hope in hell of stopping the enemy plane. Their fate was sealed. After all they had been through they were going to be pipped at the post. Suddenly he grinned at his mental use of the English expression. "Well, old buddy, a short life, but a good one!" he murmured half aloud, "And make a pretty corpse." Down below, Sergeant Hands, who seemed resigned to his fate too, said, "Roll on death and let's have a friggin' go at the friggin' angels. *Here I friggin' well come, St Peter!*"

So they waited, each man wrapped up in his own thoughts, whatever they were, young men waiting to die in a conflict they only half understood. They were the best that England could provide. Their like wouldn't be seen again.

"*Hals und Beinbruch,*"* the bomb-aimer sang out happily. "Here we go, skipper. This time we sink the bastards."

"This time we sink the bastards," the *Oberleutnant* echoed the bomb aimer's words enthusiastically. He pressed the stick forward. They were going in for the kill.

The trio of white-painted Sunderlands of Coastal Command came in low. In the lead Pilot Officer Richards took in the scene below immediately. "Great balls of flaming fire!" he exclaimed, twirling the great RAF moustache which hid his boyish face, "They've got our chaps by the short and curlies. Bad show!" He pressed forward the throttles. The huge four-engined flying boat surged forward.

In the belly of the flying boat, the signaller started to flash his Aldis lamp on and off. On the bridge of the little motor-launch, Egan could hardly believe the evidence of his own eyes. He wiped them, as if he didn't trust them. But there was no mistaking that great fat-bellied shape and the four engines. It was a Coastal Command Sunderland all right and it was right behind the

---

* 'Break your neck and legs.' The German equivalent of 'Happy landings.'

unsuspecting Jerry. Were they going to be saved after all, at the very last moment? It hardly seemed possible.

In the Heinkel Hartung watched the launch get larger and larger. The bomb-aimer was still whispering into his ear over the intercom. But the pilot was no longer taking any notice of the bomb-aimer's instructions. He had done this so often before, over Poland, France, Holland, Jugoslavia . . . he didn't need some pipsqueak of an NCO, still wet behind the ears, to tell him what to do. "*Hinein Onkel Otto!*" he chortled a little crazily. "Up him, Uncle Otto!"

Another voice seemed to be on the intercom now, screaming something which drowned out the gentler, patient tones of the bomb-aimer. Hartung took no notice. One of the noncoms had panicked. They always did. That's why they were NCOs. After all, what had his old father, the General, always maintained? "In Prussia, a gentleman starts with the rank of lieutenant." He laughed to himself. How true.

The launch now seemed to fill the whole horizon. Over the intercom, the bomber-aimer sounded off the seconds to target "*Three . . . two . . .*" Hartung's harshly handsome face contorted savagely. He could imagine the bomb-aimer peering through his sight, thumb and forefinger poised over the tit, as if his next movement was the most important in his whole life. He held his breath. It was almost there.

The Sunderland moved in totally unnoticed until the very last moment. Its turret gunner caught the Germans completely unawares. The twin-Brownings raked the length of the Heinkel's fuselage. At that range the RAF gunner couldn't miss. "*Whacko . . .* that's the stuff to give the troops!" Richards burbled, as large pieces of

213

metal began to drop from the stricken Heinkel and flutter to the sea like silver leaves. Hartung screamed as bullets tore into his back. He gasped. Desperately, the black mist threatening to overcome him, he fought the controls. Sobbing, his blood spurting from a dozen wounds, he attempted futilely to keep the Heinkel airborne.

"The Jerry kite's going down!" Richards cried. "There'll be a noggin for every man in this crew tonight!. We'll turn the mess upside down!"

He stopped short. The Heinkel fell out of the sky. "God bless my soul!" the boy behind the big moustache said, as if suddenly he had realised what he had done. "God bless my soul!"

Epilogue

From P.R. Egan, Lt Col (Retd), DSO, MC, VD, CD.

My granddaughter Clare (the one from Buffalo) says that to write this after over half a century has passed is a 'load of balls' (her expression). Who wants to know? Clare might be outspoken in the coarse modern fashion, but she's no dummy (again to use her expression). She's read her modern history. According to Clare, the raid on St Nazaire was strictly propaganda. It didn't affect the outcome of the war one iota. "It's simply" (her words) "a dreary footnote to the history of World War Two."

She comes up to see her ageing grandpop in the home every three months – for which I'm truly grateful – *weather permitting*, in winter. It's one hell of a hardship getting out of Buffalo and travelling north in the snow. She brings a breath of fresh air into this place; and if the nurses don't like her bringing me cigars and the odd quart of bourbon, she's more than likely to tell them to "go and stuff it" (or words to that effect). Me and the rest of the old farts in my ward like that. We talk about the look on Sister Aggie's sour puss for days afterwards.

But back to St Nazaire. You write to ask what I thought of the 'great raid', as the survivors, who didn't take part in that balls-up at Dieppe in August later that year, call

215

it. Well, *I* thought it worthwhile. Perhaps not an account of that *Tirpitz* business. What did happen to the frigging *Tirpitz*, Mr Harding? But because we proved ourselves as *men*, those of us who came back.

That afternoon as we sailed into Falmouth remains as one of the high points of my life. You Limeys really did us proud. I didn't know up to then that you had it in you. You know what they say about you, 'The English take their pleasures sadly.' Not that afternoon. There we were, a beat-up heap of a stolen Kraut boat, heavy with dead and dying, crawling along at two knots at the most, shipping water all the time so that in the end we were lucky to make the anchorage before we finally sank. And they were cheering us, the navy boys, the merchant marine sailors, even the thieving dockies, who nobody trusted; and the whistles were blowing and the air raid rattles and the factory sirens were shrilling away. One helluva noise! But I can tell you, Mr Harding, it brought tears to my eyes then as a kid. It still does 50 years on, confined to a wheelchair, dutifully swallowing the crappy medicine that Sister Aggie shoves down my throat three frigging times a day.

I know what Clare, my granddaughter, will say when she finally reads this (with a bit of luck, I'll have croaked it by then). "What a load of bullshit! Who remembers that guy in the kilt with his bow and arrow – shades of frigging Robin Hood? And that other little guy, Hands, the old sweat as you call him, Grandpop, and all the rest of 'em? *They died for nothing and, grow up, Grandpop, willya, nobody frigging well remembers – why should they.*"

Well, I do, Mr Harding, I certainly do. I see them every day that dawns – see them when they were young and full of piss and vinegar, as we used to say. Hell, I know they

216

could be my grandkids if they were alive today. But they aren't. Still, I see them, the brave words they shouted, the – I'd better shut up here, Mr Harding, or they'll be saying I'm going ga-ga again. I've already heard sourpuss Sister Aggie whispering to that dyke friend of hers in the lab, "I'm certain the old Colonel's exhibiting the first symptoms of Alzheimer's" They'll have me in the funny farm yet, Mr Harding. Ha, ha!

Yes, there's no denying it. I can still see them, their faces strained and serious. The sudden clatter of a Jerry machine-gun like some kid running a stick along a length of railings. Then the first wounded coming back, eyes wide and wild, arms outstretched like blind men feeling their way and the still, khaki-clad bodies crumpled in the shell holes – the price of victory. And their pals plodding on, helmets tilted at a cocky angle, their 'fag ends', as they called them, stuck behind their right ears. Then all of them turning into ghosts, vanishing into the brown, drifting smoke of war, hobnailed boots soundless, the guns muted, the cries of pain, surprise, rage, triumph dying away to nothing, echoing down the long tunnel of time . . .

A sombre thought, Mr Harding, eh? But here comes Sister Aggie pushing that goddam cart of hers with the 'down boy' pills. Now I really will shut up. 'Bye and thanks for remembering us, and St Nazaire all those years ago.

Peter Egan, Happy Days Nursing Home,
Ontario, Canada
November 1996.